GEEK ZODIAC

COMPENDIUM

JAMES F. WRIGHT

+

JOSH ECKERT

T H E
G E E K   Z O D I A C   C O M P E N D I U M

Copyright © 2013 by James F. Wright & Josh Eckert
All Rights Reserved.
Published by Geek Zodiac, LLC (USA)

For information, contact: info@geekzodiac.com

2013 HARDCOVER EDITION
PUBLISHED BY GEEK ZODIAC LLC (USA)

Cover & Layout Design by Josh Eckert

ISBN 978-0-9838188-5-4
NON FICTION
1st Printing

w w w . g e e k z o d i a c . c o m

Library of Congress Control #1-1015037661
Library of Congress Cataloging-in-Publication Data
Wright, James F.
Geek Zodiac/ James F. Wright & Josh Eckert
Summary: "A Bible to the Geek Zodiac Univers" --Provided by the publisher.
ISBN 978-0-9838188-5-4
1. Fantasy--Fiction. 2. Superheroes--Fiction. 3. Comics--Fiction.
(more categories)
I. Josh Eckert. II. Title.

D E D I C A T I O N S

To Mom, who made sure we read; to Pa, who made sure we
read comics; and to Walter, who let me read his.

To everyone at Geoffrey's Comics, who supported me and this
project.

To Rosemary, Janice, Sree and Konrad, who pushed me like no
one has before.

To the memory of Dr. Keiko McDonald, who always believed
in me, even when I didn't. I hope we came through with flying
colors.

And to Josh, whose friendship, honesty and talent made this
whole thing worthwhile... and an absolute blast. When you're
making comics in the big leagues, don't forget about me.

- James

To Mom and Dad and Jeremy, for being my first captive
audience and feeding all my creative fires over the years.

To James, for having ideas so good they demand to be brought
to life. You showed me what true collaboration is. If you're not
in the big leagues before me, there's no justice in this biz.

To Lori, for your love and patience during my long hours. I've
limped to so many finish lines with you at my side.

To Claire, because the thought of you being in the world and
reading this is too exciting to bear. With love, from the past,
my little Pirate. Or is it Daikaiju?

- Josh

CONTENTS

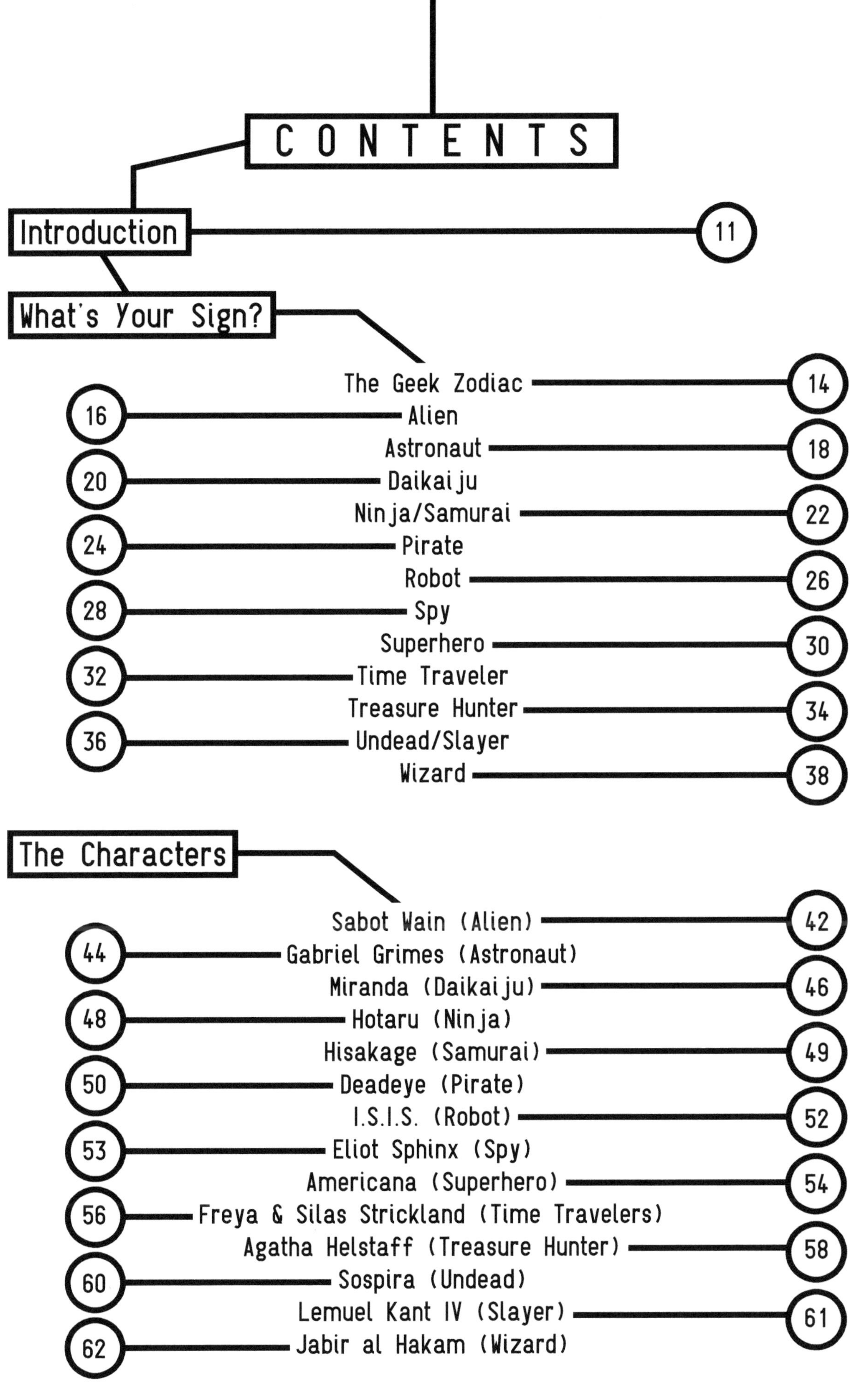

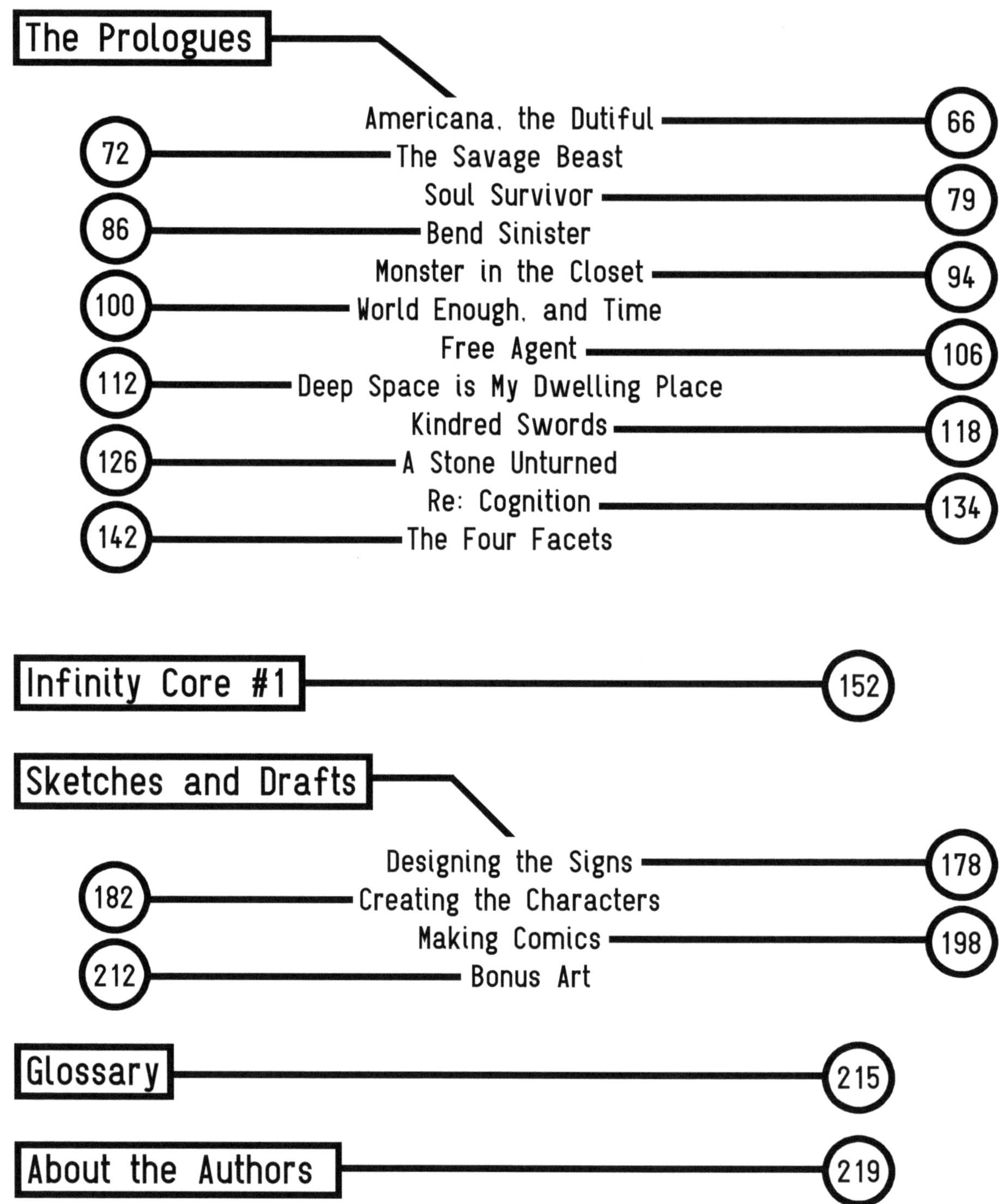

THE FOUR FACETS

  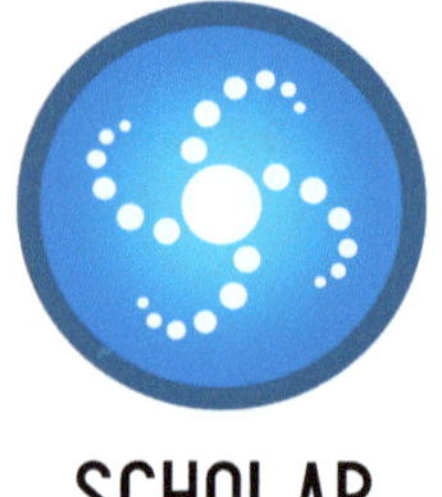 

FIGHTER   ROGUE   SCHOLAR   STRANGER

THE FOUR ASPECTS

BODY   SPIRIT   MIND   SOUL

THE FOUR ELEMENTS

EARTH   FIRE   WATER   AIR

I N T R O D U C T I O N

It's still hard to believe this book even exists.

When we came up with the idea for the Geek Zodiac back in the spring of 2011, it was really just as a lark. We were bored and got to thinking about how the stuff we were into as kids (and as adults, we're not ashamed to admit)—ninjas and robots and spies and superheroes—had a tendency to operate in cycles. From there it was a matter of assigning each of these interests to one of twelve categories, and once the ball starting rolling we had an all-new zodiac chart on our hands.

We thought it was simply something our friends would get a kick out of and nothing more, but when we released it into the aether of the Internet, it was like wildfire. People were sharing it and talking about it and rejoicing (or complaining) about what their new zodiac sign revealed. The chart was and always will be the major draw of the project, but we asked ourselves what else we could do with it. As longtime fans of four-color stories and sequential art, the answer was obvious: make comics.

Here we had a wholly original idea on which to base characters and a series of stories, not beholden to any previous heroes or continuities, and we began to experiment first with a series of prologues and later with a full-fledged comic. The prologues served both as a means for us to get a grasp on the characters and also to explore the various genres and storytelling tropes tied to each sign. There was a '60s-styled spy double-cross, a '40s-inspired superhero tale, a treasure hunter from the '30s and more. With the prologues well in hand, we set these characters loose in the *Geek Zodiac: Infinity Core* comic to see their adventures come to life.

And here we are. Again, it's hard to believe this book exists. An idea born from a listless weekend has yielded so much more than we could ever have imagined. This has been a labor of love and a labor of joy, the sheer act of creating something new and fun and original, where the enthusiasm never once abated.

But the best part? The best part is that this is only the beginning.

James F. Wright
Geek Zodiac co-creator
Los Angeles, CA

WHAT'S
YOUR
SIGN
?

THE GEEK ZODIAC

1923 The burial chamber of King Tutankhamun is unsealed, revealing the golden sarcophagus.

TREASURE HUNTER
+ Adventurous. Cultured. Quick Thinker
- Greedy. Loner. Cavalier with laws/rules

NINJA/SAMURAI
+ Loyal. Deferential. Level headed
- Unemotional. Subservient. Violent

1910 The director of the most enduring and lauded samurai, or jidaigeki, films is born.

ASTRONAUT
+ Bold. Team oriented. Precise
- Untethered. Distant. Controlling

1969 The first people in the history of mankind land on the moon.

SPY
+ Confident. Patriotic. Desenrascanço adept
- Duplicitous. Selfish. Remorseless

1908 The author of arguably the most famous spy in literature is born.

TIME TRAVELER
+ Punctual. Perceptive. Cosmopolitan
- Regretful. Distracted. Chaotic

1895 The most well-known science-fiction novel popularizing time travel is published.

DAIKAIJU
+ Center of attention. Big hearted. Scientific
- Destructive. Lonely. Misunderstood

1954 The giant monster, or kaiju, genre of film emerges in a big way from Japan.

2019 2007 1995 1983 1971 1959 1947 1935 1923 1911

2018 2006 1994 1982 1970 1958 1946 1934 1922 1910

2017 2005 1993 1981 1969 1957 1945 1933 1921 1909

2016 2004 1992 1980 1968 1956 1944 1932 1920 1908

2015 2003 1991 1979 1967 1955 1943 1931 1919 1907

2014 2002 1990 1978 1966 1954 1942 1930 1918 1906

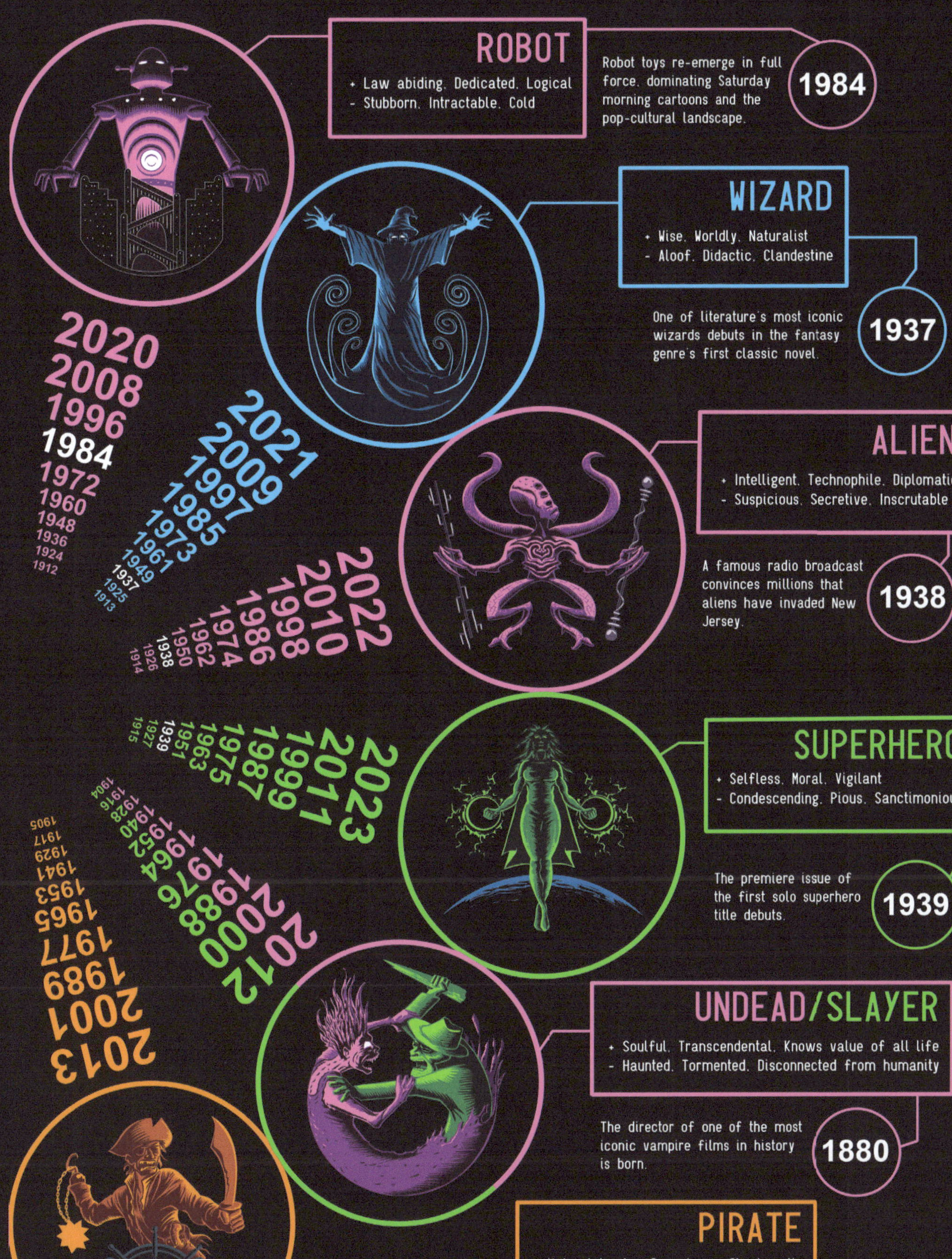

ROBOT
+ Law abiding. Dedicated. Logical
- Stubborn. Intractable. Cold
Robot toys re-emerge in full force, dominating Saturday morning cartoons and the pop-cultural landscape.
1984

WIZARD
+ Wise. Worldly. Naturalist
- Aloof. Didactic. Clandestine
One of literature's most iconic wizards debuts in the fantasy genre's first classic novel.
1937

ALIEN
+ Intelligent. Technophile. Diplomatic
- Suspicious. Secretive. Inscrutable
A famous radio broadcast convinces millions that aliens have invaded New Jersey.
1938

SUPERHERO
+ Selfless. Moral. Vigilant
- Condescending. Pious. Sanctimonious
The premiere issue of the first solo superhero title debuts.
1939

UNDEAD/SLAYER
+ Soulful. Transcendental. Knows value of all life
- Haunted. Tormented. Disconnected from humanity
The director of one of the most iconic vampire films in history is born.
1880

PIRATE
+ Natural leader. Bon viveur. Charismatic
- Restless. Quick to anger. Untrustworthy
One of the most popular pirate stories begins serialized publication.
1881

2020
2008
1996
1984
1972
1960
1948
1936
1924
1912

2021
2009
1997
1985
1973
1961
1949
1937
1925
1913

2022
2010
1998
1986
1974
1962
1950
1938
1926
1914

2023
2011
1999
1987
1975
1963
1951
1939
1927
1915

2013
2001
1989
1977
1965
1953
1941
1929
1917
1905

2012
2000
1988
1976
1964
1952
1940
1928
1916
1904

THE GEEK ZODIAC

YEAR OF THE
ALIEN
1926 - - 1938 - - 1950 - - 1962 - - 1974 - - 1986 - - 1998 - - 2010 - - 2022

The Alien overflows with ambition and the need to succeed in every way.

You can manipulate others with ease due to your heightened intelligence and need to get to the top of your desired field. You are intensely stubborn, enigmatic and suspicious.

The Alien's inability to trust comes from a lack of deep self-belief. You know you are smart, but is that really so? Are you as sharp as the next person, or is there knowledge being kept from you? This can make you own worst enemy and completely ruthless in this dogged desire to acquire what you may feel is being hidden from you.

You should know that you will always get what you want and reach where you need to be in life, because your tenacity and desire for success will not allow you to achieve anything less.

As an Alien, you will do well to learn to share and trust in yourself more, so that those around can respond in kind. What you put forth is what you get back, but your inherent stubbornness and self-absorption can stop you from discovering this about yourself.

POSITIVE ATTRIBUTES:
Intelligent, Technophile, Diplomatic
NEGATIVE ATTRIBUTES:
Secretive, Suspicious, Indiscernible
ELEMENT: Air
FACET: Stranger
ASPECT: Soul

INFINITY CORE CHARACTER: Sabot Wain (p. 44)

SOURCE YEAR: 1938
A famous radio broadcast convinces millions that aliens have invaded New Jersey.

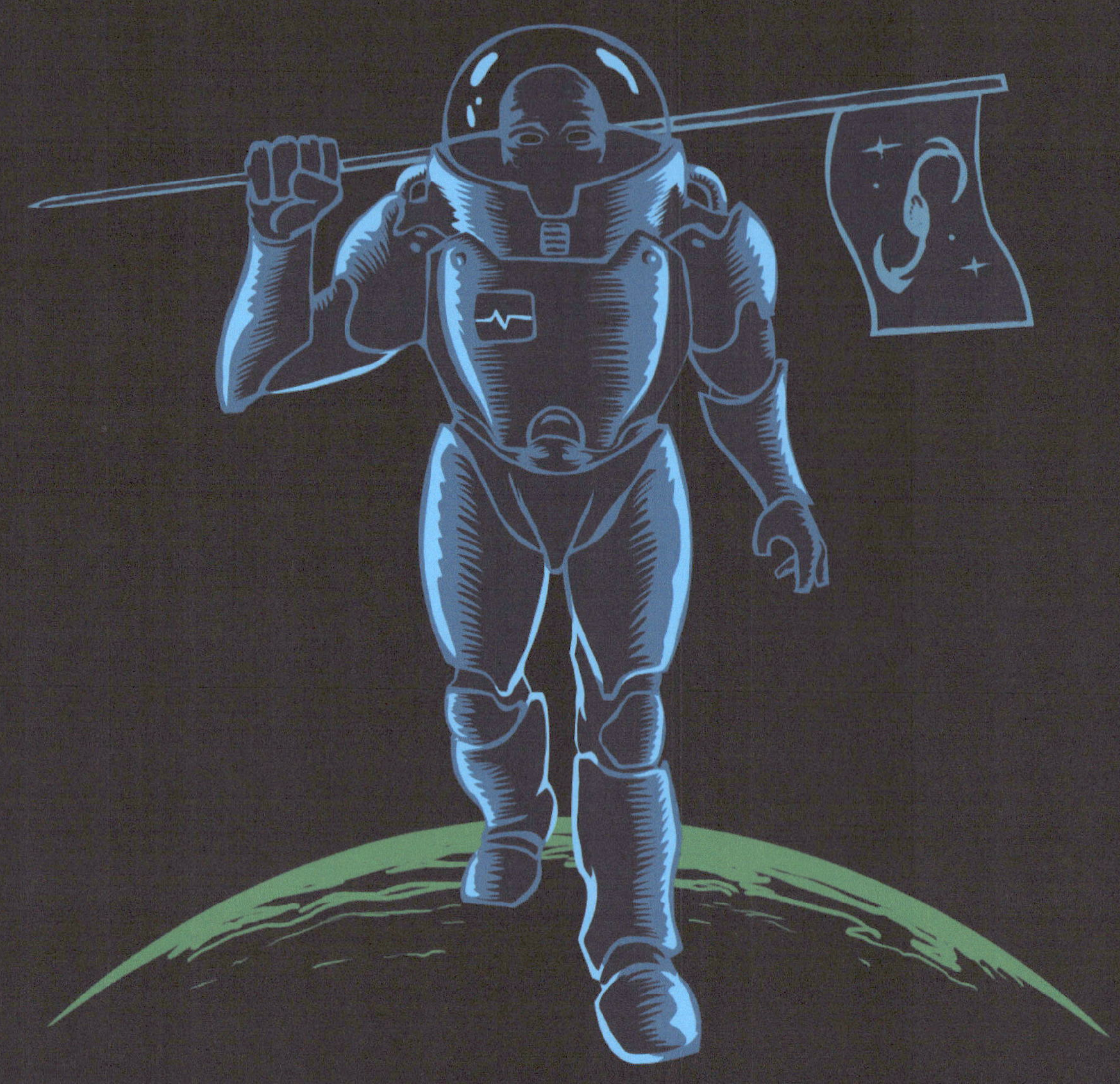

YEAR OF THE
ASTRONAUT

The Astronaut spends so much time in the realm of the greater universe that you can tend to become detached from the real world. You have your own agenda and constantly think outside the box to fulfill it.

You prefer to work things out in your own precise methods that you developed and finessed over time. Although you will happily work with others for the greater good, you need to be allowed your independent thought process and path to answers. As an Astronaut, you tend to be forward thinking, but you need at times too "get real" if you want to be understood and accepted as part of the team.

The kindness that you are capable of is legendary, but you dispense it from a distance because the Astronaut has no time for drama and emotional upheaval—you are here to change the world and that is where your focus and intent will always lie. Your destiny as an Astronaut is to be able to come down to earth and happily embrace all that makes you different, so you can make practical use of your unique talents.

Your destiny is the search for that faith in yourself to act now with the knowledge you already have, rather than waiting for a day to know for sure, a day that may never come.

POSITIVE ATTRIBUTES:
Bold, Team-oriented, Precise
NEGATIVE ATTRIBUTES:
Untethered, Distant, Controlling
ELEMENT: Water
FACET: Scholar
ASPECT: Mind

INFINITY CORE CHARACTER: Gabriel Grimes (p. 46)

SOURCE YEAR: 1969
The first people in the history of mankind land on the moon.

YEAR OF THE
DAIKAIJU
1918 - - 1930 - - 1942 - - 1954 - - 1966 - - 1978 - - 1990 - - 2002 - - 2014

A Daikaiju is a formidable opponent in life since your attention to detail, methodical learning and pure stubbornness will not allow you to give in, no matter what or who you are up against.

Those born under this sign are extremely sensitive to the words and actions of others and this creates a huge amount of compassion and humanity within. Although you have a strong sense of what is right and wrong, your own feelings and interpretations of events can often get in the way of what is truly going on.

As a Daikaiju, communication and the ability to say what you are feeling does not come readily. This is often interpreted by the outside world as sullenness and lack of interest in the feelings of others.

Once someone crosses you, there is no going back. The ability to forgive and forget is not part of your natural make up and this is what compels a Daikaiju to fight on until the death.

Daikaiju's destiny is never to "bend without breaking," which ends up being the your worst enemy as well as your greatest ally.

POSITIVE ATTRIBUTES:
Center of attention, Big hearted, Scientific
NEGATIVE ATTRIBUTES:
Destructive, Lonely, Misunderstood
ELEMENT: Air
FACET: Stranger
ASPECT: Soul

INFINITY CORE CHARACTER: Miranda (p. 48)

SOURCE YEAR: 1954
The giant monster, or kaiju, genre of film emerges in a big way from Japan.

YEAR OF THE
NINJA * SAMURAI
1922--1934--1946--1958--1970--1982--1994--2006--2018

Never doubt that there are always two identities to deal with when you interact with a Ninja/Samurai. Both can be deadly and the ability to switch from one to the other is instant and often imperceptible to the naked eye. An idealist at heart, your confidence and ability to bluff your way through life can cover up a much more devious and proud alter-ego, which you must always guard against.

You are a multi-talented person who can skip from talent to gift with ease. However, learning to master your skills is something you don't often pay enough attention to. Being the "jack of all trades and the master of none" is often a Ninja/Samurai's downfall in life. So, until you learn to focus, your determination and talents can easily be wasted.

Acting impulsively makes you exciting yet unpredictable to be around which can be dire and even deadly for those who choose to oppose you and/or align themselves with you.

As a Ninja/Samurai, it is your destiny in life to become the master of your thoughts and actions and to use your versatility and diverse talents for the greater good, not just for your own entertainment and pleasure.

POSITIVE ATTRIBUTES:
Loyal, Deferential, Level-headed
NEGATIVE ATTRIBUTES:
Unemotional, Subservient, Violent
ELEMENT: Fire / Earth
FACET: Rogue / Fighter
ASPECT: Spirit / Body

INFINITY CORE CHARACTERS: Hotaru and Hisakage (p. 50)

SOURCE YEAR: 1910
The director of the most enduring and lauded samurai, or jidaikei, films is born.

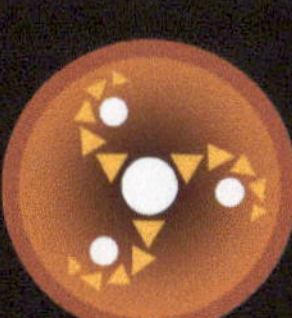

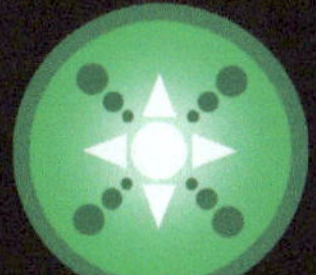

YEAR OF THE
PIRATE
1917 - - 1929 - - 1941 - - 1953 - - 1965 - - 1977 - - 1989 - - 2001 - - 2013

The Pirate always has eyes on the treasure but head in the clouds.

Others are naturally drawn to your sign by your charisma, creativity and love of life, though they are also wary that you cannot always be trusted. The world of fantasy and freedom pulls at the Pirate constantly, therefore your actions and experiences can take you away from what "should" be done into what you would like to see done.

You're seen as restless and adventurous on one hand and unscrupulous and conniving on the other. For you the end justifies the means. You rush through life encapsulated in your own world of imagination and fantasy.

Focusing on the task at hand will often only work for a Pirate if there is something in it for him/her—whether it is excitement or material gain. So, although your charm and ability to express yourself make you a natural leader, you tend be a fence-sitter, and then suddenly sometimes you take sides impetuously.

The Pirate's destiny is to harness ambition and imagination, which, when they fall in sync, take you where you need to go in life for all the right reasons.

POSITIVE ATTRIBUTES:
Natural Leader, Bon viveur, Charismatic
NEGATIVE ATTRIBUTES:
Restless, Quick to anger, Untrustworthy
ELEMENT: Fire
FACET: Rogue
ASPECT: Spirit

INFINITY CORE CHARACTER: Deadeye (p. 52)

SOURCE YEAR: 1881
One of the most popular pirate stories begins serialized publication.

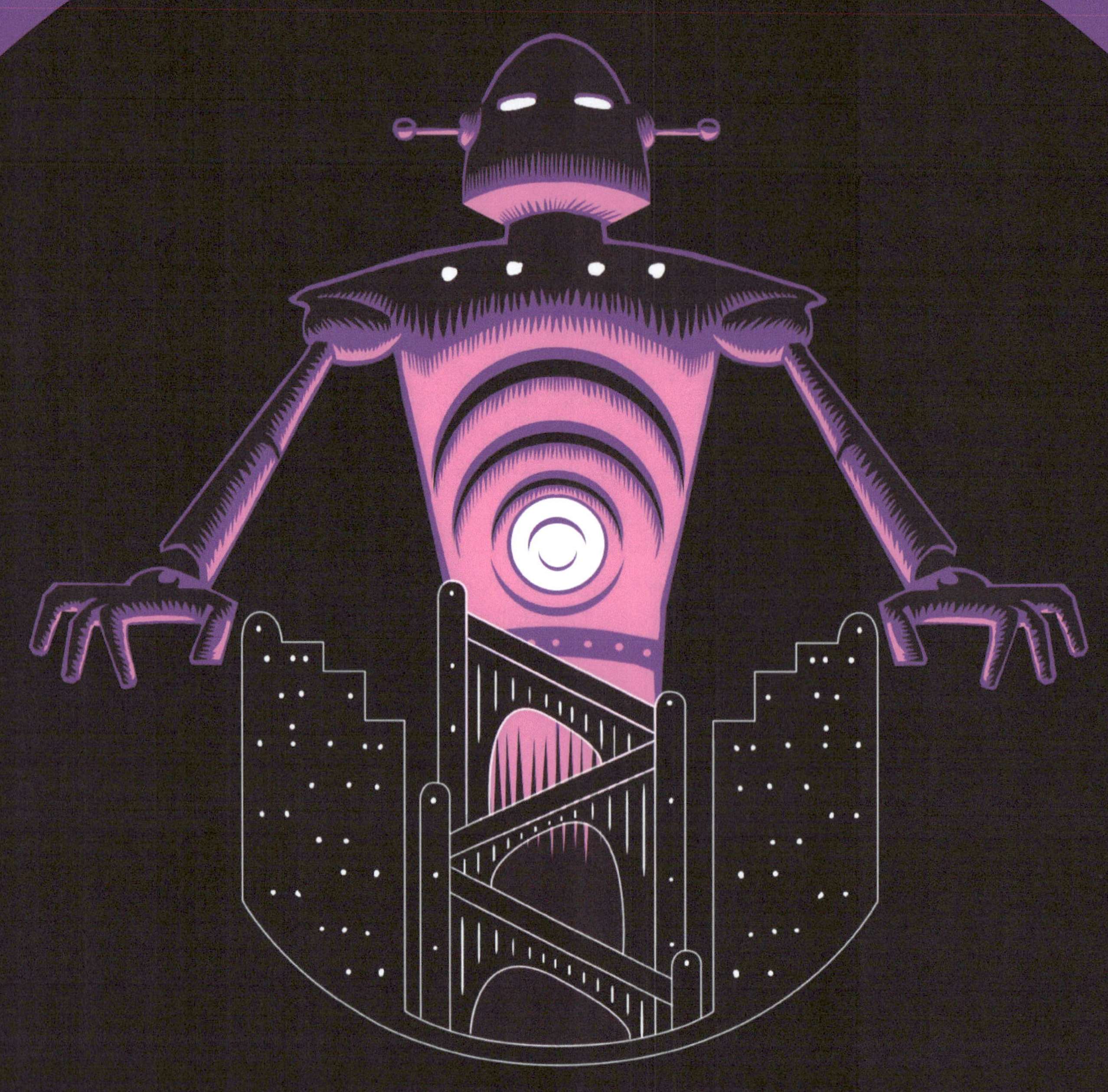

YEAR OF THE
ROBOT
1924 -- 1936 -- 1948 -- 1960 -- 1972 -- 1984 -- 1996 -- 2008 -- 2020

Being a Robot is about being perfect. There is little room for failure or not measuring up to the task at hand.

You are intensely logical, grounded and organized, and as such you are the perfect candidate in a work environment—whether it is assisting someone, being an employee, or fighting for a cause.

Intensely hard on yourself, failure is not an option, especially perceived failure in the eyes of others. You have high expectations for yourself and those around you, treating others in the same uncompromising way you treat yourself. Therefore, the Robot often tends to have unrealistic goals, which results in little compassion for anyone who cannot deliver at the highest level.

A Robot is very sensible and a lover of rules, boundaries and structure. Technology and science can be places where you feel at more at home rather than the world of imagination, creativity and drama.

Your blessing and a curse as a Robot is that you want to be perfect, accomplish your goals without stress or fear of failure, and you never can and will give less than a hundred percent.

POSITIVE ATTRIBUTES:
Law abiding, Dedicated, Logical
NEGATIVE ATTRIBUTES:
Stubborn, Intractable, Cold
ELEMENT: Air
FACET: Stranger
ASPECT: Soul

INFINITY CORE CHARACTER: I.S.I.S. (p. 54)

SOURCE YEAR: 1984
Robot toys re-emerge in full force, dominating Saturday morning cartoons and pop cultural landscape.

YEAR OF THE
SPY
1920--1932--1944--1956--1968--1980--1992--2004--2016

The Spy operates undercover in every way. You love playing games, and often what you see is not what you get and you relish this.

Deeply secretive, intense and ruthless, you will do whatever it takes to find your power in life and take no prisoners along the way.

The Spy hates to be victimized by anyone or anything, yet there is a sensitivity underneath all the subterfuge. Meaning, you feel things a lot more deeply than you let on.

Once crossed, the Spy will move heaven and earth to seek vengeance. You have a sign that others want to have as an ally and never as your enemy unless they are prepared to be as dastardly and devious as you can be.

Highly intelligent and infinitely resourceful, the Spy does not stop until the mission is complete and the objective is reached. You never have any doubt that you can achieve anything you set your mind to, whatever the cost.

Your destiny as a Spy is to use your skill and intelligence to uncover what will benefit the entire Universe and not just your own secret desire for power and success.

POSITIVE ATTRIBUTES:
Confident, Patriotic, Resourceful
NEGATIVE ATTRIBUTES:
Duplicitous, Selfish, Remorseless
ELEMENT: Fire
FACET: Rogue
ASPECT: Spirit

INFINITY CORE CHARACTER: Eliot Sphinx (p. 55)

SOURCE YEAR: 1908
The author of arguably the most famous spy in literature is born.

YEAR OF THE
SUPERHERO
1927 - - 1939 - - 1951 - - 1963 - - 1975 - - 1987 - - 1999 - - 2011 - - 2023

You are not called a Superhero for nothing. You expect from those a round you nothing less than what you expect from yourself.

The Superhero has a huge need for glory, kudos and respect, but as we know pride can often come before a fall.

You will fight tirelessly with formidable strength for all that you believe in, showing vigilance, dedication and loyalty that is second to none. However, being able to see things from another perspective is often just not in your DNA.

Although you have a big heart, the Superhero has even bigger ego. Therefore, even as you give much of yourself to others, you will always take care of #1—yourself—first and foremost. Drama is often a great part of your life as also the need to express who you are and what you are feeling, but this is what makes the Superhero seem ten feet tall and bulletproof in a crisis.

Your destiny as a Superhero is to save the world, but your dilemma will always be to do so with an open mind and because it is the right thing to do, and not for all the appreciation and glory that this will bring you personally.

POSITIVE ATTRIBUTES:
Selfless, Moral, Vigilant
NEGATIVE ATTRIBUTES:
Condescending, Pious, Sanctimonious
ELEMENT: Earth
FACET: Fighter
ASPECT: Body

INFINITY CORE CHARACTER: Americana (p. 56)

SOURCE YEAR: 1939
The premiere issue of the first solo superhero title debuts.

YEAR OF THE
TIME TRAVELER
1919--1931--1943--1955--1967--1979--1991--2003--2015

As a Time Traveler it is your journey in life to understand what lies between the lines and between the worlds.

Intelligent, honest and forthright you have the ability to lead others, to pioneer new discoveries and to be at the forefront of scientific breakthroughs and original thoughts.

Your passion and forthrightness can however cause you to lose sight of what is for the highest good of all concerned and may be interpreted by some as arrogance and self-serving if not kept in check.

Your greatest asset is your mind and your ability to cut to the chase. It draws people to you as their leader and protector. Compassion and understanding for how others think and act does not come easily to you as you prefer to operate along the lines of "it's my way or the highway!"

You have unlimited energy and passion for your goals in life but this can cause much chaos and disruption when your vision is limited to only what you can see for yourself.

Ruled by the head rather than the heart, a Time Traveler's destiny is to lead the way using perception and brilliance rather than impetuousness and ego.

POSITIVE ATTRIBUTES:
Punctual, Perceptive, Cosmopolitan
NEGATIVE ATTRIBUTES:
Regretful, Distracted, Chaotic
ELEMENT: Water
FACET: Scholar
ASPECT: Mind

INFINITY CORE CHARACTERS: Silas & Freya Strickland (p. 58)

SOURCE YEAR: 1895
The most well-known science fiction novel popularizing time travel is published.

YEAR OF THE
TREASURE HUNTER
1923 - - 1935 - - 1947 - - 1959 - - 1971 - - 1983 - - 1995 - - 2007 - - 2019

The Treasure Hunter is the Peter Pan of the Geek Zodiac. To you life is one big adventure—the more excitement and variation you can pursue and create in your life the better.

You can think on your feet, making quick decisions that almost always lead you to your treasure. Your ability to live and operate in the moment means that you often prefer to work alone on your quests, saving your need for others for social occasions.

As a Treasure Hunter, you absorb information from all that you read and hear, and you usually master all that you choose to learnto the point of brilliance. But with this comes a need to be in control of all that goes on around you, as well as a need to judge those you feel may not possess the same intelligence and mastery as you do.

If you are born under this sign you will never be content because you are always looking to explore and expand your horizons. It is the Treasure Hunter's destiny to acquire and deliver that formidable bounty of knowledge to all who wish to learn and not to discriminate between who is worthy of this and who is not.

POSITIVE ATTRIBUTES:
Adventurous, Cultured, Quick thinker
NEGATIVE ATTRIBUTES:
Greedy, Loner, Cavalier with laws/rules
ELEMENT: Fire
FACET: Rogue
ASPECT: Spirit

INFINITY CORE CHARACTER: Agatha Helstaff (p. 60)

SOURCE YEAR: 1923
The burial chamber of King Tutankhamun is unsealed, revealing the golden sarcophagus.

YEAR OF THE
UNDEAD / SLAYER
1916 - - 1928 - - 1940 - - 1952 - - 1964 - - 1976 - - 1988 - - 2000 - - 2012

Being an Undead/Slayer is all about finding balance within yourself and within your life in every way, every day.

This sign swings from extreme to extreme to find harmony. You can be a people-pleaser one minute and a domineering rule-maker the next. Uncertainty, lack of self-belief/confidence and the need to fit in hinders the Undead/Slayer's ability to empathize with others. Instead of just accepting these weaknesses, you need to understand them and let them go.

Your love for the arts creates a wonderful outlet for your passion and creativity, which you use to hide your true feelings. This is because you are not the type to raise your hand or put yourself "out there." Consequently, you let opportunities for success and accomplishment pass you by.

The Undead/Slayer has much internal power plus much spiritual power, but often you are uncertain how and where to use this, which causes indecisiveness and the inability to make choices, preventing you from positively affecting the lives of others.

As an Undead/Slayer your destiny is to discover the honor and balance between what is in your best interests and what is in the best interests of those around you.

POSITIVE ATTRIBUTES:
Soulful, Transcendental, Knows value of all life
NEGATIVE ATTRIBUTES:
Haunted, Tormented, Disconnected from humanity
ELEMENT: Air / Earth
FACET: Stranger / Fighter
ASPECT: Soul / Body

INFINITY CORE CHARACTERS: Sospira & Lemuel (p. 62)

SOURCE YEAR: 1880
The director of one of the most iconic vampire films in history is born.

YEAR OF THE
WIZARD
1925--1937--1949--1961--1973--1985--1997--2009--2021

As a Wizard, you move through life absorbing and gathering knowledge from everyone you encounter, making your wisdom and intuition second to none.

Your ability to care and show compassion to all living things is without judgement and has no limits. Consequently, you can also be gullible and overly accepting of others. But the Wizard is by no means stupid, and can see through the pretense into the souls of friends and foes. Your loyalty and understanding run deep and it takes much to break either, but once broken, they can rarely ever be repaired.

To a Wizard the feelings and well being of others is paramount. You will often put such external needs well ahead of your own. To this end, you have a need to retreat into your own space at times, recoup your energy and absorb all that you have seen, felt and heard.

The Wizard's destiny is to learn to care and empathize from a position of detachment and to know that no amount of wisdom can help change the future when you put yourself first, and see your own needs as being the most important in the Universe.

POSITIVE ATTRIBUTES:
Wise, Worldly, Naturalist
NEGATIVE ATTRIBUTES:
Aloof, Didactic, Clandestine
ELEMENT: Water
FACET: Scholar
ASPECT: Mind

INFINITY CORE CHARACTER: Jabir al Hakam (p. 64)

SOURCE YEAR: 1937
One of literature's most iconic wizards debuts in the fantasy genre's first classic novel.

THE CHARACTERS

SABOT WAIN

ALIEN

NAME: Sabot Wain
SIGN: Alien
FACET: Stranger
AGE: Ageless
ERA: Timeless
NATIONALITY: Nationless
ETHNICITY: Alien
ELEMENT: Air
ASPECT: Soul
Blood Type: None

SABOT WAIN IS THE HARBINGER of The Entrope, an ancient entity born from the creation of the universes and that seeks to return all worlds to darkness. One of the first four beings to stand (and fall) against The Entrope. Sabot Wain was transformed into its emissary, tasked with finding universes for its master to destroy. Though unable to openly defy The Entrope due to the entity's control over her, Sabot

Wain actively searches for those universes containing elements capable of stopping the ancient force and to free her from servitude.

When astrophysicists Dr. Silas and Freya Strickland's experiments with the four unstable Empyrean particles (believed to be the base elements of existence) expose the couple to the particles' unique energies and tear open a portal in space and time, Sabot Wain is certain she has found the world she as long been seeking. Emerging from this portal, Sabot Wain attempts to warn the scientists to gather "The Infinity Core" before it's too late, but The Entrope's programming takes over and Sabot Wain decimates the laboratory and lays waste to the Stricklands' colleagues.

While their exposure to the Empyrean particles spares Silas and Freya from Sabot Wain's wrath, the two try to stop the invader from further destruction, but their struggle is in vain...

Sabot Wain throws Freya into the portal, sending her far into Earth's past, and Silas, in hopes of saving

his wife, leaps in after her, himself transporting to a different era in history. The alien then goes about its mission of preparing the way for The Entrope by altering planet Earth, but in the deep recesses of her heart where her master cannot see, the real Sabot Wain is content that she has set in motion events that may well elad to the end of The Entrope. Though a villain on the surface, Sabot Wain is a reluctant one, incapable of exercising free will as she tries to free herself, and the multiverse, from bondage.

GABRIEL GRIMES

NAME: Gabriel Grimes
SIGN: Astronaut
FACET: Scholar
AGE: 27
ERA: 1970s
NATIONALITY: American
ETHNICITY: African-American
ELEMENT: Water
ASPECT: Mind
Blood Type: AB

GABRIEL IS A GENIUS-LEVEL astrophysicist who is as impressive at the controls of air- and spacecraft as he is at a university blackboard. He made his name with his Theorem of the 12 Worlds, which posited 11 other Earth-like planets inhabiting the same location as ours, spread across 11 other planes of existence. In spite of all this, and in spite of the fact that he works at one of the secret bases for AEGIS*, he's been passed over for missions both public and private because of his race. But when a rendezvous in space with an artifact from

one of the other 11 worlds goes wrong, Grimes gets the call to lead the rescue mission. Not only does he successfully bring the stranded astronauts home, he is contacted by the alien artifact, which changes Grimes and his spacecraft forever, bonding man and machine in an unforeseen manner. Grimes' superiors have plans to extract the alien influence (and his new man-machine interface) from him, possibly killing him in the process. With his old employer after him, he goes on the run...

Administration for the Exploration of Galactic and Interstellar Space.

miranda

NAME: Miranda
SIGN: Daikaiju
FACET: Stranger
AGE: 13
ERA: 1950s
NATIONALITY: Brazilian
ETHNICITY: Afro-Brazilian
ELEMENT: Air
ASPECT: Soul
Blood Type: O

MIRANDA WAS THE SUBJECT of various invasive experimental procedures. Her trials, however, came at the hands of fugitive Nazi scientists hiding out in the remote forests of Brazil, as they hoped to create a new form of biologicial weapon. Though the youngest of the twelve orphaned girls at the center of this tragedy, Miranda possessed the most mental fortitude, and she soon discovered that as a result of these experiments she's able to transform into "Caliban," a massive, destructive monster - a daikaiju - and thus made short work of her captors. Unfortunately, she was unable to sustain this form and, upon reverting to her 13-year-old form, was captured by Brazilian authorities with a mind toward further experimentation.

But there's more to Miranda than a Jekyll-and-Hyde girl who transforms into a giant monster. The other eleven victims of the fateful experiment were all linked together physically and psychically, but they all perished leaving Miranda to keep her consciousness alive within her, such that not only do they speak to her and advise her, but also that the transformation into "Caliban" is an explosion of the psychic energy within her manifesting in the physical realm.

HOTARU

NAME: Hotaru
SIGN: Ninja
FACET: Rogue
AGE: 18
ERA: 15th Century
NATIONALITY: Japanese
ETHNICITY: Asian
ELEMENT: Fire
ASPECT: Spirit
Blood Type: B

SEPARATED AT BIRTH as part of a devil's bargain between warring ninja and samurai clans, the twins Hotaru and Hisakage grew up with no knowledge of the others' existence. Hotaru, the elder, was brought up in the wilderness by a secret clan of kunoichi, (female ninja). Hisakage, the younger, was raised by his distinguished samurai father and trained in Bushido since childhood. Unfortunately, the twins' personalities and strengths do not lie in their respective worlds. Despite her prowess in stealth and misdirection, Hotaru is deemed too com-

bative and too much of a firebrand to be entrusted with serious missions. This earns her the name Hotaru (Firefly). Hisakage, meanwhile, is expected to lead his samurai clan upon his father's death, but has no heart for war or bloodshed, seeking peaceful resolution to any conflict. Though he carries

HISAKAGE

a sword as a step toward appeasing his father, he refuses to draw it, fighting with it sheathed.

The chief goal of Hotaru's ninja clan was getting the scroll of the 12 Daimyo, a listing of the movements and strengths of 12 samurai leaders, while the goal of Hisakage's samurai clan was to get the

NAME: Hirakawa Hisakage
SIGN: Samurai
FACET: Fighter
AGE: 18
ERA: 15th Century
NATIONALITY: Japanese
ETHNICITY: Asian
ELEMENT: Earth
ASPECT: Body
Blood Type: A

Scroll of the 12 Shadows, detailing the location of the 12 ninja clans in the area. Hotaru's master and Hisakage's father hoped their young charges would be able to help obtain these documents, but soon saw there is no future for them in their respective clans. The twins were then exiled into the wilderness. But fate has other plans for them, and as they wander the woods trying to figure out what comes next, they happen upon each other...

DEADEYE

NAME: Edmund "Deadeye" Pike
SIGN: Pirate
FACET: Rogue
AGE: 32
ERA: 16th Century
NATIONALITY: English
ETHNICITY: Caucasian
ELEMENT: Fire
ASPECT: Spirit
Blood Type: B

CAPTAIN EDMUND DEADEYE PIKE once counted himself among Queen Elizabeth's most trusted triumverate, a trio that also included her spymaster Sir Francis Walsingham and famous captain Sir Francis Drake. Much like Drake, Pike was a sailor of near superhuman acclaim, yet while Drake was ostensibly the face of the British Empire at sea, Pike acted as the Empire's dirty hands keeping it alive. Loyal almost to a fault, when tasked by Walsingham with infiltrating the Spanish fleet, in order to acquire a mystical nautical star chart - The Map of the 12 Islands - he accepted without hesitation. Unfortunately, during his mission, Walsingham died, and Pike's hated rival Drake took over all operations. Where before his mission was strictly undercover, with Drake in charge he was made out to be a traitor, and he was stripped of all land and titles due him. What's more, his very name (a name shared by his wife and children) became tainted throughout the annals of British history.

The name Pike became so distasteful that its bearers couldn't find honest work anywhere - so they turned to dishonest work. Pike's descendants changed their surname to Helstaff - a sly nod to the name of his ship, The Hell's Staff - and became first a family then a legacy of thieves.

I.S.I.S.

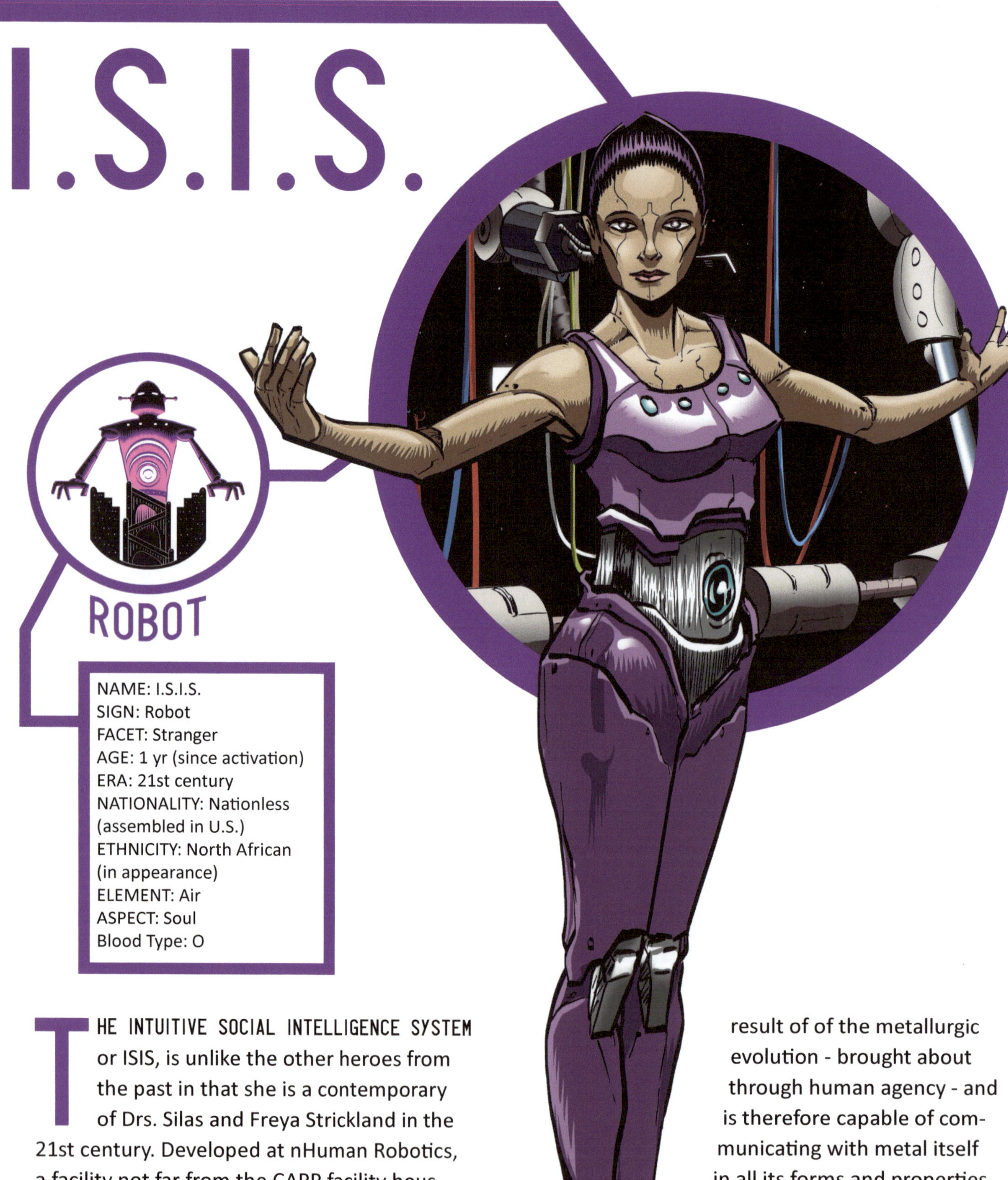

ROBOT

NAME: I.S.I.S.
SIGN: Robot
FACET: Stranger
AGE: 1 yr (since activation)
ERA: 21st century
NATIONALITY: Nationless
(assembled in U.S.)
ETHNICITY: North African
(in appearance)
ELEMENT: Air
ASPECT: Soul
Blood Type: O

THE INTUITIVE SOCIAL INTELLIGENCE SYSTEM or ISIS, is unlike the other heroes from the past in that she is a contemporary of Drs. Silas and Freya Strickland in the 21st century. Developed at nHuman Robotics, a facility not far from the CAPP facility housing the Stricklands' Empyrean particle experiments, ISIS represents the event horizon of the Singularity, the most advanced blurring of the line between human and machine. What makes her truly unique, however, is that she is the end result of of the metallurgic evolution - brought about through human agency - and is therefore capable of communicating with metal itself in all its forms and properties. in addition to this, she possesses an intuitive understanding of all technology and computer systems.

ELIOT SPHINX

SPY

NAME: Eliot Sphinx
SIGN: Spy
FACET: Rogue
AGE: 30 (real age unknown)
ERA: 1960s
NATIONALITY: Unknown
ETHNICITY: Caucasian
ELEMENT: Fire
ASPECT: Spirit
Blood Type: B

SPHINX IS THE VERY DEFINITION OF MERCURIAL. He's the super spy that all alleged super spies aspire to be. In fact, no on even knows his real name: Eliot Sphinx is simply what he's been known as most recently. While his age is listed as 30, he can be younger or older as the situation requires. He's intimately familiar with the customs and histories of countless nations, and if there is a language spoken he can probably speak it. A triple-agent adept at the double cross, he is by no means flashy but rather virtually invisible. Such that you'd likely forget him minutes after having met him. Unfortunately all of these skills were rendered moot when his employer double-crossed him, selling a list with his name - and those of eleven other key agents - to the highest bidder. To save his skin, Eliot has to get his hands on the List of the 12 Operatives.

SUPERHERO

NAME: Dana Danner (nee Ruth Rochester)
SIGN: Superhero
FACET: Fighter
AGE: 23
ERA: 1940s
NATIONALITY: American
ETHNICITY: Caucasian
ELEMENT: Earth
ASPECT: Body
Blood Type: A

DANA DANNER (NEE RUTH ROCHESTER) made her living as a pin-up model in the early 1940s, under the stage name of Americana. Her popularity helped bolster the confidence of U.S. troops serving in the European and Pacific theaters during WWII, and her photos decorated many a barracks wall or bomber's nose art. But there's more to Americana than just a pretty face: she was also a superhuman super-soldier capable of flight, as well as increased strength, speed and endurance. She used these talents to engage in hands-on support of the war effort in Europe and North Africa. However, this was not merely an act of national pride, but a means of self-preservation. As on of the surviving child test subjects of a government program attempting to turn the concept of patriotism into a physical construct. Dana's abilities

and well-being were directly tied to the real and perceived prosperity and strength of the U.S. When the war ended, she sought to retire to civilian life in hopes of finding out who she really was. To do so would require her to track down the other 11 children who were part of the initial experiments that made her. Unfortunately, with the rise of Communism, the U.S. wanted to keep her active. Dana refused and soon found herself an enemy of her own country.

With her abilities connected psychogeographically to the Union, as the nation changes so do her powers. As a girl during the Great Depression, for instance, she developed a form of photosynthesis to draw sustenance from the sun as a response to a diminished food supply. The 21st Century into which she arrives shifts her abilities yet again.

FREYA & SILAS STRICKLAND

NAME: Dr. Freya | Silas Strickland
SIGN: Time Traveler
FACET: Scholar
AGE: 45 | 50
ERA: 21st Century
NATIONALITY: American
ETHNICITY: Afro-Asian | Caucasian
ELEMENT: Water
ASPECT: Mind
Blood Type: AB

WHEN RESEPECTED ASTROPHYSICISTS Drs. Freya and Silas Strickland discovered what came to be known as the Empyrean particles, it was heralded as one of the great breakthroughs in science. Dubbed "fighter," "scholar," "rogue" and "stranger" for their behavior, the four unstable particles were believed to represent the base elements of existence. The two scientists and their team sought to unlock the mysteries of the universe by smashing the four particles together in a large collider. But when their experiment went wrong, Silas leapt in to salvage it, exposing himself to the unique particles.

Freya, fearing for her husband, leapt in to save him, throwing her own life at the mercy of the Empyrean particles. Shortly afterward, the collider exploded, tearing open a rift in space and time, and from whih emerged the alien, Sabot Wain.

The alien spoke a few cryptic words about "gathering the 12," before grabbing Freya and throwing her into the rift. Fearing for his wife's safety, Silas jumped in after her...

To her surprise, Freya found herself not in the 21st century but aboard a ship in the 16th century, inhabiting the body of female captain Bethany Britannia. Meanwhile, Silas wound up in the 12th century Alexandria, Egypt, also inhabiting a different body - this one of a prisoner named Malik. Now they must learn how to navigate their time periods, and figure out a way to return to her own time, if such a thing is possible. And they must find out who these mysterious 12 are before it's too late...

AGATHA HELSTAFF

NAME: Dr. Agatha Helstaff
SIGN: Treasure Hunter
FACET: Rogue
AGE: 24
ERA: 1930s
NATIONALITY: Mexico-England
(dual-citizenship)
ETHNICITY: Hispanic/Caucasian
ELEMENT: Fire
ASPECT: Spirit
Blood Type: B

AGATHA IS AN ACCOMPLISHED TREASURE HUNTER and adventurer
who uses her considerable knowledge in archaeology,
anthropology and linguistics to track down and acquire
priceless artifacts for museums and cultural sanctuaries.
The descendant of a long line of rogues and thieves (the Pirate,
Edmund "Deadeye" Pike, is her direct an-cestor). Agatha is well-versed
in her family's tricks of the trade, yet finds herself seeking to use these
skills as a force for good and for cultural understanding. Her very
raison d'etre as a treasure hunter stems from her desire for the Helstaff
name to be viewed with positivity rather than scorn. The holy grail of her
quest is an ancient tablet known as The Cycle of the 12 Kingdoms. Though believed
by many to be a map to 12 lost civilizations, Agatha instead sees it as depicting the

destruction of the world, with each Kingdom representing the 12 archetypes of existence. What she doesn't know is that this tablet is the means by which she will travel to the future to help save the world from The Entrope.

SOSPIRA

NAME: Sospira
SIGN: Undead
FACET: Stranger
AGE: 100 (but 18 in appearance)
ERA: 19th Century
NATIONALITY: Italian-born
ETHNICITY: Caucasian
ELEMENT: Air
ASPECT: Soul
Blood Type: O

SOSPIRA, THE YOUNGEST of a small coven of sorceresses known as the Sisters of Sorrow, traveled the countryside with her family preying on the men who would seek to do them harm. Lemuel's demon-hunting father dragged him - a promising musician with no heart for the family business - along on a mission with his men to eliminate the feared Sisters of Sorrow. Unfortunately for the hunters, they were unprepared for the Sisters, who began laying waste to them in horrific fashion.

LEMUEL KANT IV

NAME: Lemuel Kant IV
SIGN: Slayer
FACET: Fighter
AGE: 17
ERA: 19th Century
NATIONALITY: German-Italian
ETHNICITY: Caucasian
ELEMENT: Earth
ASPECT: Body
Blood Type: O

However, Lemuel Kant IV managed to sway the heart of Sospira with his music, and she protected him and his father from her Sisters' wrath. When it was over, Sospira's Sisters banished her from their coven for daring to spare the lives of men, while Lemuel's father, too ashamed to face his son, denounced him as his own and left him. Thus bereft of family, Sospira and Lemuel joined forces in hopes of finding the root cause of the animosity between the Sisters and the demon hunters. The root which rests in an ancient book. The Tome of the 12 Spirits...

JABIR AL-HAKAM

NAME: Jabir al-Hakam
SIGN: Wizard
FACET: Scholar
AGE: 55
ERA: 12th Century
NATIONALITY: Egyptian
ETHNICITY: Arab
ELEMENT: Water
ASPECT: Mind
Blood Type: AB

JABIR AL-HAKAM ("THE JUDGE") is a polymath and scientist in the classical mold: his interests and proficiencies are one and the same, proving himself equally adept at everything from mathematics and astronomy to meteorology and alchemy. His understanding of the physical world is so vast and daunting that many have deemed him a wizard - some out of respect and other pejoratively. Operating in the 12th century Alexandria, Jabir spends his days testing his hypotheses and instructing the youth of his town,

in hopes that they will appreciate the world as he has. One of his alchemical adventures opened up his consciousness, and in a trancelike state he composed a mystical Zodiac Chart. This chart was comprised of 12 new signs, based around four chief facets: scholar, fighter, rogue and stranger. The emir of Alexandria at the time, Saladin, believed that this chart would give its bearer the power to see the future - a crucial advantage during the Second Crusade - and sought the means to have it for himself. Jabir, however, knew that his chart held a greater power: to save the world from destruction. But to do so he would need to gather the avatars of all 12 signs...

THE PROLOGUES

From the fall of 2011 to the end of summer 2012, James and I ran the following series of webcomics under the title, The Continuum. Using the Geek Zodiac as our source of inspiration, we created 14 original characters and tied them together in an epic time travel adventure story. Each character represented a different era, culture, and genre of storytelling. It was a massive undertaking, so we made it more manageable by releasing these prologue comics, which show us what each of the characters were doing before entering the larger narrative (Geek Zodiac: Infinity Core). Through our work on these prologue comics, James and I grew so much as a creative team and I think there is a noticeable evolution in his writing and my artwork. We're very proud of what's in these pages, though there are quite a few cringe-inducing panels for me.

A couple things to note: since we didn't nail down the overall series plot until after publishing the prologues, there is no alien prologue and the Time Traveler's prologue has no relevance to what you see in Infinity Core. However, for the sake of this book we wanted to make sure it was seen because it still makes a great stand-alone story and hints at where we originally wanted to steer this thing.

- Josh E.

THE SUPERHERO

FEBRUARY 1944. OVER SCHWEINFURT GERMANY

KEEP YOUR EYES PEELED, BOYS

AND YOU KEEP YOUR SHIRT ON, CUTTER.
YOU'VE GOT A FLEET OF ACES AT YOUR SIDE.
HEY, WAITAMINIT YOU GUYS--

WHO TOLD COLE HE WAS AN ACE? DID THE DEFINITION CHAN--
BRAKAKAKA
LEAVE IT TO THE NAZIS TO RUIN A PERFECTLY GOOD JOKE.

DON'T LET 'EM HIT THE FORTRESS!
KACK ACK ACK ACK ACK A
BOOM
BRAPNBRAP
I GOT 'IM.
ACK ACK ACK ACK ACK ACK
LITTLE HELP, HERE, GUYS?
THAT MAKES TWO OF US!
HANDS FULL AT THE MOMENT.
ACTUALLY, IT MAKES THREE OF US.
★ THEN WHAT SAY WE ★ EVEN THE ODDS SOME?
SHABOOM KABLAM

YOU WERE EXPECTING CARMEN MIRANDA?
IT'S TRUE. SHE DOES LOOK BETTER IN PERSON.
THE CONTINUUM PRESENTS
AMERICANA
THE SUPERHERO
written by JAMES F. WRIGHT
art by JOSH ECKERT

Meet AMERICANA the SUPERHERO

Alias: Dana Danner   Age: 23

Blood Type: Invincible

Merits: Moral, Vigilant, Selfless
Demerits: Pious, Sanctimonious, Condescending

Likes: Doc Savage
Dislikes: The Shadow

Strengths: Super Strength, Flight, Acoustic Guitar

Stats:
Truth   18
Justice   18
Goodness   18
Gee-Whiz   16
Street Smarts 4

1.
Look out, Nazis. This firecracker is reporting for duty.

2.
Sorry, Hitler. You're just not her type

PRESIDENT ROOSEVELT SAYS
"I WANT HER FOR THE U.S. ARMY!"
EVERYONE'S GOT AMERICANA FEVER!

LEMUEL KANT IV

THE SLAYER

VENICE, ITALY
LATE 19TH CENTURY
WHAT DID YOU CALL THEM, SIGNOR KANT? ...FATA MORGANA?
FELL SHE-SPIRITS WHO ONCE LURED SAILORS TO THEIR DEATHS, AND NOW HAVE TAKEN UP RESIDENCE IN THE CANALS OF VENICE.
WITH MY OWN EYES I SAW THEM, SIGNOR KANT. MY DAUGHTERS. BUT WITH MY HEART...?
IN MY HEART I KNEW IT WAS NOT THEM. THAT THEY DROWNED AGES AGO.
IT'S JUST BEEN SO QUIET HERE BY MYSELF. WHAT I WOULDN'T GIVE TO HEAR THEIR--
giggle
I CALL THIS ONE, "TO THE FAIREST."
giggle
LEMUEL!

SOFIA... OFILIA... BELLADONNA... YOU CAME BACK.
THE FATA MORGANA! OPEN YOUR EYES, SON. THEY'RE--
FELL SHE-SPIRITS. REVENANTS. DEMONS. YES, I KNOW.
BUT I'VE TURNED THE TABLES-- MY SONG HAS ENSNARED THE SIRENS.
WHAT MAGIC IS THIS?
MUSIC, FATHER.
LAMENTABLY, I HAVEN'T MASTERED THIS TUNE YET.
AND SOONER OR LATER I'LL HIT A FALSE NOTE--
TWANG
--AND THE SPELL WILL BE BROKEN.

AND SOMETIMES... COUGH ...SOMETIMES...

SOMETIMES...
I CAN FIND THE SONG AGAIN.
AND BY CHANGING THE TUNE JUST SLIGHTLY...
WHAT– WHAT ARE YOU?

I'M WHAT HAPPENS WHEN YOU REALIZE YOU DON'T HAVE TO DESTROY EVERYTHING YOU DON'T UNDERSTAND.
SNAP
I'M A MUSICIAN.
I'M YOUR SON.
THE CONTINUUM:
LEMUEL KANT IV
THE SLAYER
in
"THE SAVAGE BEAST"
written by
JAMES F. WRIGHT
art by
JOSH ECKERT

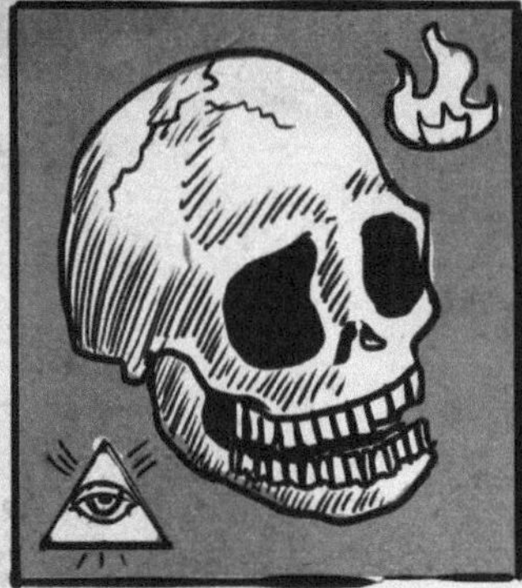

MIRACLES DIABLERIES MUSIC

Name: Lemuel Kant
Blood Type: O
Age: 19

Merits
Soulful,
Transcendental,
Knows Value of All Life

Demerits
Haunted,
Tormented,
Difficulty Relating to Humanity

Era: Late 19th Century

Likes: Serenading

Dislikes: False Notes

Strengths
Exorcism,
Demonology,
Crossword Puzzles

Stats
Stakes: 17
Silversmithy: 16
Holy Water: 14
Garlic Cultivation: 13
Whimsy: 5

WITNESS THE UNTHINKABLE

DESCENDANT OF THE WORLD FAMOUS KANT DEMON HUNTERS COMMUNES WITH THE UNDEAD

LEMUEL KANT THE IV
THE SLAYER

THE UNDEAD

NORTHERN ITALY.
LATE 19TH CENTURY

"HAVE I EVER TOLD YOU THE STORY OF THE SISTERS OF SORROW, CHILD?

"EIGHT YEARS AGO, THREE ROMA SISTERS-- HEALERS ALL-- WERE BETRAYED BY THE VERY PEOPLE THEY ONCE SERVED.

"FEW THINGS STIR UP A MOB LIKE A TRAGEDY. AND A WOMAN TO BLAME IT ON.

"THERE WAS BEAUTIFUL CORDELIA, THE ELDEST.

"MELANCHOLY LUCIA, THE MIDDLE SISTER.

"AND, FINALLY, IMPERIOUS ESMERELDA, THE YOUNGEST.

"A RUMORED SUCCUBUS CHARGED WITH ENSORCELLING THE VIRTUOUS.

"BRANDED A BANSHEE AND ACCUSED OF DRIVING STALWART MEN TO DESPAIR.

"ACCUSED OF WITCHCRAFT AND KILLING THE HARVEST.

WHAT ARE WE TO DO NOW?
AND WITH NO MAP? WHERE ARE WE TO GO?
AFTER ALL WE DID FOR THEM, I CAN'T BELIEVE THEY WOULD TURN ON US.
"AND WHILE THE SISTERS ESCAPED UNWOUNDED, THE SAME COULD NOT BE SAID FOR ESMERELDA'S PRIDE.
BURNING DOWN OUR HOME, DESTROYING OUR WORK, CHASING US OUT OF TOWN...
WHAT THEY DID TO US WAS UNFAIR, BUT WE SHALL BALANCE THE SCALES.
IF THEY THINK US AGENTS OF DARKNESS, THEN LET US PROVE THEM RIGHT.
LET US SHOW THEM WHAT TRUE EVIL LOOKS LIKE.

"FUELED BY ESMERELDA'S ANGER, THEY DELVED INTO THEIR CONSIDERABLE KNOWLEDGE...
"..REVERSING THEIR HEALING LORE BACK ON ITSELF, EXPOSING ITS DARK INVERSE.
"BUT FORCES OF SHADOW ARE BEYOND MAN'S KEN AND SOON THE SISTERS FELL PREY TO THEIR OWN HUBRIS.
"CORDELIA WAS TRANSFORMED INTO A SUCCUBUS
"LUCIA A BANSHEE.
"AND ESMERELDA, HER RANCOR SUPPLANTED BY FEAR, TURNED INTO THE WITCH OF HER ACCUSERS.
"BUT THE ABYSS HAD YET SOMETHING MORE TO GIVE THEM, AT AN EQUALLY HEAVY PRICE.

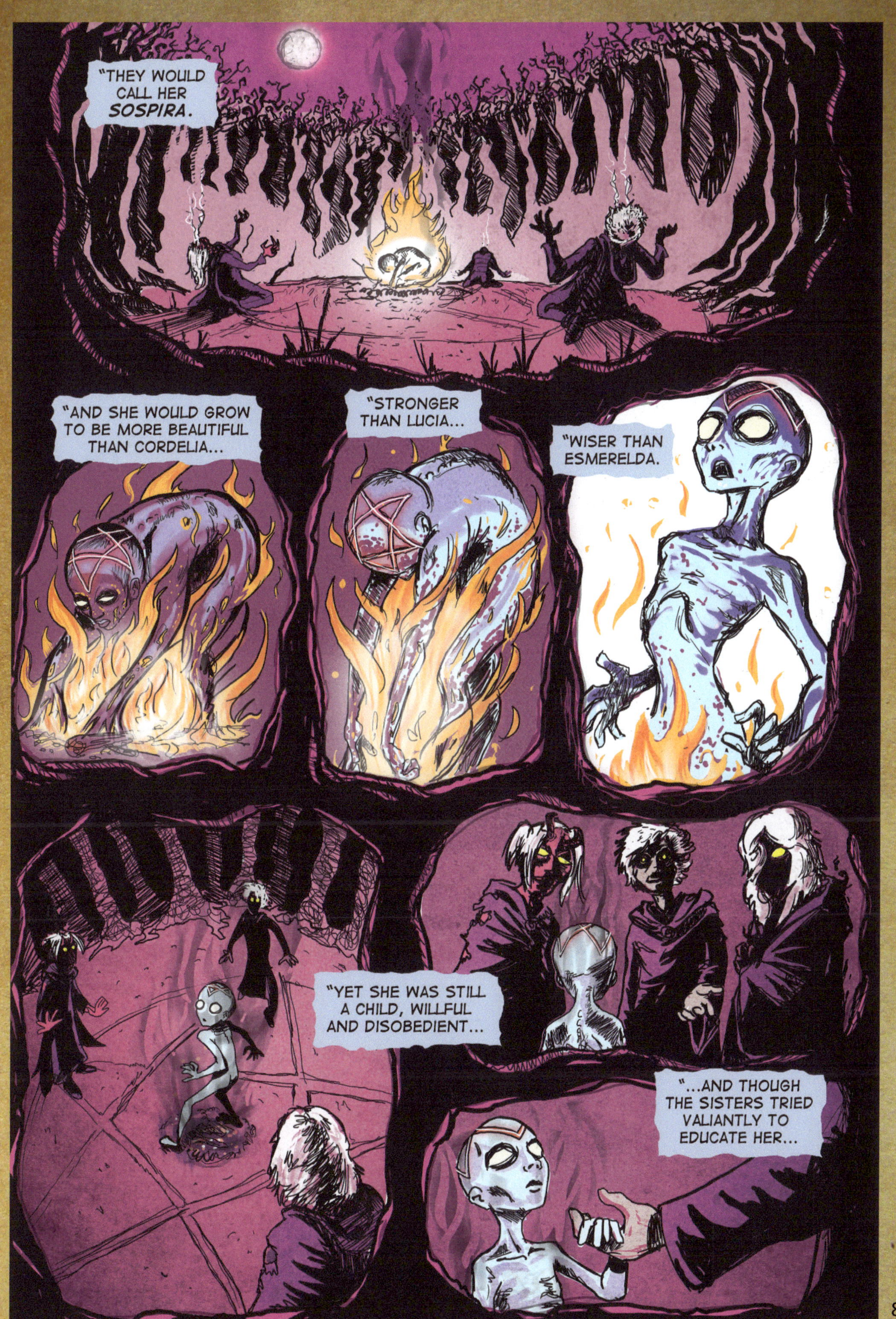

"THEY WOULD CALL HER SOSPIRA.
"AND SHE WOULD GROW TO BE MORE BEAUTIFUL THAN CORDELIA...
"STRONGER THAN LUCIA...
"WISER THAN ESMERELDA.
"YET SHE WAS STILL A CHILD, WILLFUL AND DISOBEDIENT...
"...AND THOUGH THE SISTERS TRIED VALIANTLY TO EDUCATE HER...

EIGHT YEARS LATER
...IT WAS CLEAR SHE WOULD ONE DAY REBEL AGAINST THEM.
ISN'T THAT RIGHT, SOSPIRA?
OH, ESMERELDA.
THE THINGS I'VE DONE FOR YOU ALL OVER THE YEARS NO LOVING SISTER WOULD ASK OF ANOTHER.
THE CONTINUUM PRESENTS
SOSPIRA
THE UNDEAD
NOW ALL I ASK IS THAT YOUR IMMINENT JOURNEY TO HELL BE AS PAINFUL AS POSSIBLE.
WRITTEN BY JAMES F. WRIGHT
DRAWN & COLORED BY JOSH ECKERT
INKED BY KEVIN JOHNSON

DEMERITS
DISCONNECTED from HUMANITY
HAUNTED, TORMENTED, TRAPPED
MERITS
Soulful, Transcendental,
Knows Value of all life
LIKES
DARIO ARGENTO
DISLIKES
FRANK CAPRA
ERA LATE 16th CENTURY
AGE TIMELESS
BLOOD TYPE REGRET
NAME
Sospira
the UNDEAD
STATS
STRENGTHS
POSSESSION
INTANGIBILITY
ARIAS
MELANCHOLY: 15
GRIEF: 16
SORROW: 16
WOE: 13

DEADEYE
THE PIRATE

OFF THE COAST OF ENGLAND. LATE 16TH CENTURY
"I TELL YOU, SIR WALSINGHAM, WE WERE OUTNUMBERED, OUT-GUNNED."
"THEN WHAT DID YOU DO?"
"THAT'S JUST IT..."
PIRATES. BLOODY COWARDS.
INFORM THE PASSENGER, MR. COLES.
"...I DID NOTHING."
SIR, THE CAPTAIN WANTED ME TO INFORM YOU.
IT'S PIRATES, SIR. FOUR BRIGANTINES, UNLIKELY TO GIVE ANY QUARTER
I SUPPOSE THAT DOES COMPLICATE MATTERS SOMEWHAT.
MY GOD! MR. COLES, COME LOOK!

HA!
LEAVE IT TO A PIRATE TO TURN ON HIS MATES.
HELL'S STAFF
HUZZAH! HUZZAH!
I DON'T KNOW WHO COMMANDS THE HELL'S STAFF...

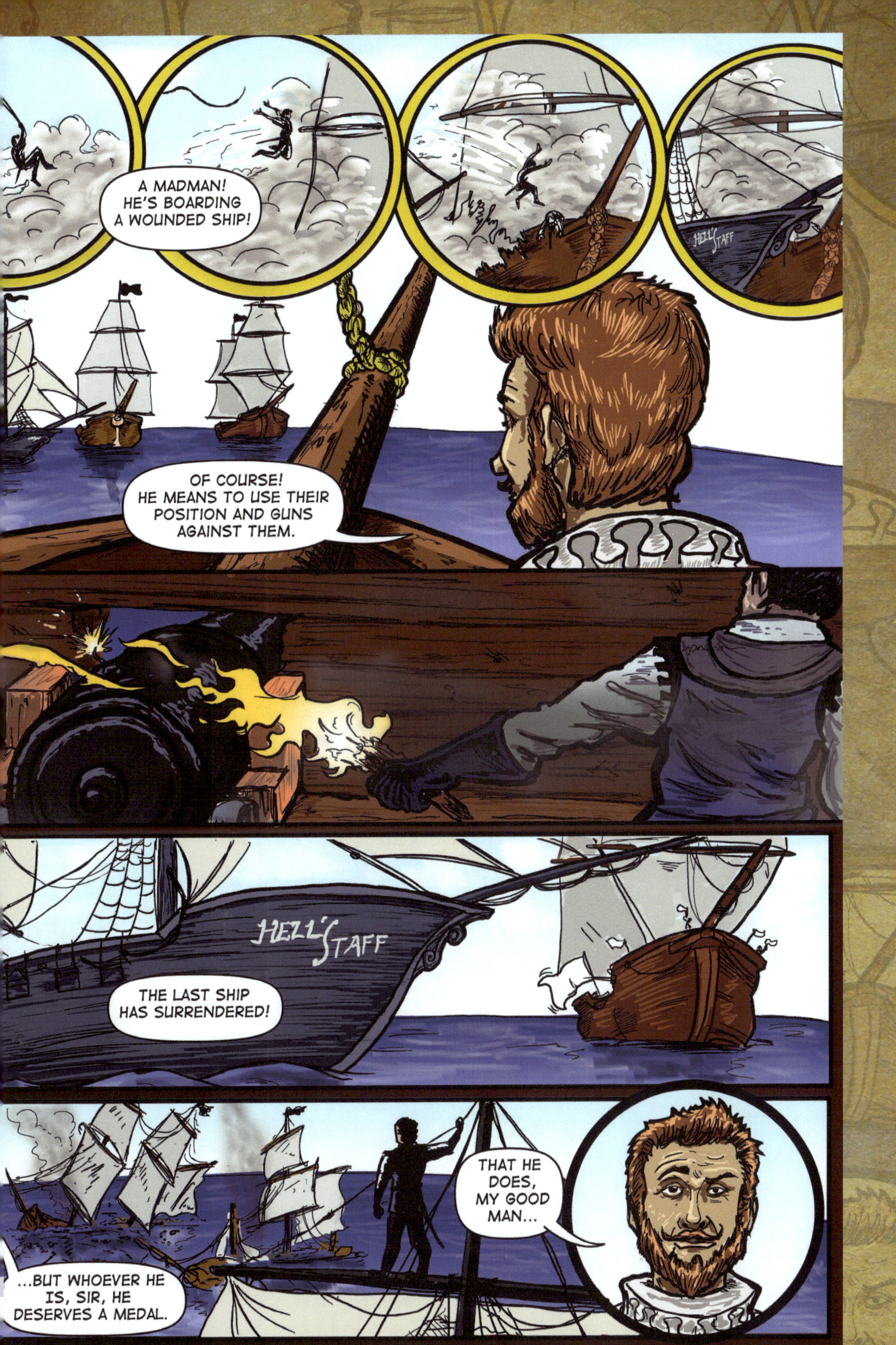

A MADMAN! HE'S BOARDING A WOUNDED SHIP!
HELL'S STAFF
OF COURSE! HE MEANS TO USE THEIR POSITION AND GUNS AGAINST THEM.
HELL'S STAFF
THE LAST SHIP HAS SURRENDERED!
THAT HE DOES, MY GOOD MAN...
...BUT WHOEVER HE IS, SIR, HE DESERVES A MEDAL.

"... AND I'LL SEE THAT HE GETS IT."
IN ALL MY YEARS I'VE NEVER SEEN ANYTHING LIKE IT.
LONDON, ENGLAND. DAYS LATER.

IF THESE PLANS HAD FALLEN INTO PIRATE HANDS...
WELL, DON'T KEEP ME WAITING. WHO WAS THIS INTREPID MARINER?
HE CALLED HIMSELF THE "BASTARD OF BRITAIN," BUT THAT IS CLEARLY NOT HIS CHRISTIAN NAME.

AND IF I MAY BE SO BOLD, SIR WALSINGHAM...
...I THINK HE SHOULD WORK FOR THE CROWN.
"THE BASTARD OF BRITAIN?"
WHY, MY GOOD SIR, HE ALREADY DOES.

SIR FRANCIS DRAKE, MY RIGHT HAND MAN, ALLOW ME TO INTRODUCE YOU TO MY LEFT...
CAPTAIN EDMUND "DEADEYE" PIKE.
THE CONTINUUM:
DEADEYE
THE PIRATE in "Bend Sinister"
written by
JAMES F. WRIGHT
pencils & colors by
JOSH ECKERT
inks by
KEVIN JOHNSON

ACTES

and Monumentes of matters moſt

ſpeciall and memorable , happenyng in the
name of Engliſhe kynges and queens agai
nſt ſubjectes of enemy ſtates on the high ſeas
from the yeare of our Lord one thouſand five
hundred and eighty to the preſent daye.

The destruction and surrender of a pirate fleet by the infamous Edmund "Deadeye" Pike

Name: Edmund Pike ~ Age: 30 ~ Era: Elizabethan ~ Blood Type: Seaworthy ~ Merits: Natural leader, Bon viveur, Charismatic ~ Demerits: Restless, Quick to anger, Untrustworthy ~ Likes: The smell of the sea ~ Dislikes: The smell of the seasick ~ Strengths: Swashbuckling, Keelhaul Survival, Eyepatch Fashion ~ Stats: Charisma: 17, Daring: 17, Navigation: 18, Nautical Engineering: 15, Rum Resistance: 3

PIRATE

THE DAIKAIJU

JULY 1956
THE AMAZON RAINFOREST
PERIGO
ALTA TENSÃO
DAMN.
WHAT IS IT, HEINRICH?
SOMETHING'S NOT ADDING UP. THERE'S A MIS-CALCULATION SOMEWHERE.
MAYBE WE SHOULD TELL THE DOCTOR. HE'LL BE INSPECTING SOON.
OH, YES. LET'S TELL DR. JOSEF BLOODY MENGELE THAT HIS MATH IS WRONG.
I'M SURE HE'LL UNDERSTAND.
COME. LET'S SEE IF WE CAN FIX THIS BEFORE HE SHOWS UP.

COME ON. WE WON'T GET ANOTHER CHANCE.
WAIT. LET ME GET MIRANDA.

FINE. SHE'S YOUR RESPONSIBILITY, CARLA.
BUT IF SHE DECIDES TO HAVE ONE OF HER FITS AGAIN--

"--SHE WON'T HAVE TO WORRY ABOUT THE NAZIS GETTING THEIR HANDS ON HER."

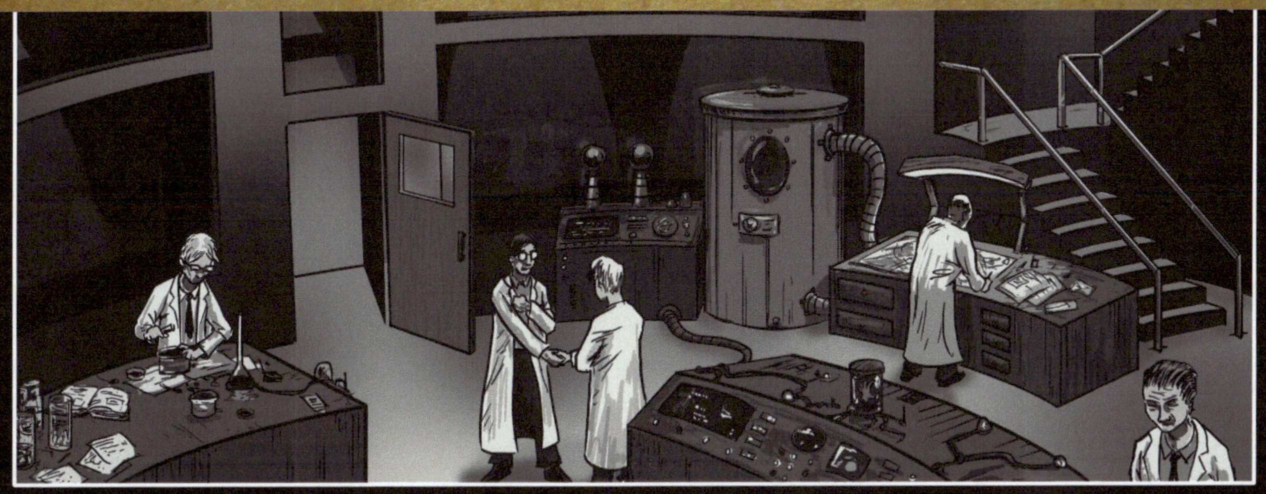

OH NO.
STAY WITH ME, MIRANDA. BREATHE.
YOU ARE NOT HAVING A FIT.

I KNOW, CARLA. THIS ONE FEELS...

"...DIFFERENT."
MIRANDA? WHAT... WHAT HAPPENED?
I'M NOT SURE--

"...BUT I THINK I LIKED IT."
THE CONTINUUM:
MIRANDA
THE DAIKAIJU
in
"The Monster in the Closet"
WRITTEN BY JAMES F. WRIGHT
ART BY JOSH ECKERT

SILAS STRICKLAND

THE TIME TRAVELER

NORTHEASTERN TECHNOLOGY INSTITUTE.
2025.
NOW.
IT'S THE AGE OLD QUESTION, ISN'T IT?
IF YOU COULD GO BACK AND DO ONE THING OVER, WOULD YOU?
SHOULD YOU?
The Freya Strickland Memorial Institute for Trans-Temporal Research
THE CRUEL IRONY IS THAT THE VERY THING YOU WANT TO CHANGE THE MOST...
6 MONTHS AGO.
...IS THE ONE THING YOU CAN'T.
...STAGE IV GLIOBLASTOMA.
I'M SORRY, DR. STRICKLAND.
IF ONLY WE'D CAUGHT IT SOONER THERE MIGHT HAVE BEEN SOMETHING WE COULD--
HANG ON. "SOONER?"
HANG ON. "SOONER?"
HANG ON. "SOONER?"
HANG ON. "SOONER?"
THIS STORY IS NOT CANON

YOU WANT TO WHAT?
I'M GOING TO USE THE PASSAGE. TO GO BACK IN TIME.
IT MAKES SENSE, FREYA. EARLY DETECTION IS KEY, AND IF I GO BACK FAR ENOUGH THE DOCTORS CAN FIND THE TUMOR SOONER.
BUT THE PASSAGE ISN'T OPERATIONAL, YET.
AND IT'S MEANT TO GO FORWARD IN TIME, NOT BACKWARD.
FOR YOU I WOULD FIND A WAY TO MAKE IT WORK.
SILAS...
... I LOVE YOU AND I LOVE THAT YOU WOULD TRY.
BUT THERE ARE TOO MANY VARIABLES IN THE PAST.
TOO MANY THINGS THAT CAN GO WRONG.
PLEASE PROMISE ME YOU WON'T.
I... I PROMISE.
THANK YOU, SILAS.
BUT SPEAKING OF THE PASSAGE, IT'S NEVER GOING TO REACH OPERATIONAL STATUS WHILE WE'RE COOPED UP IN THIS HOSPITAL...
THIS STORY IS NOT CANON

INSTITUTE FOR TRANS-TEMPORAL RESEARCH
THIS STORY IS NOT CANON
"... AND I'D RATHER SPEND MY TIME WORKING ON THAT THAN SITTING AROUND WAITING TO DIE."
AND YOU'RE SURE ABOUT THIS? YOU'RE SURE THIS IS WHAT YOU WANT?
MM-HM.
IF A CURE FOR THIS EXISTS, IT'LL BE IN THE FUTURE.
OKAY, FREYA...
... LET'S SEE WHAT THE FUTURE HOLDS.

"TO MY FAVORITE PHYSICIST...
"WHEN I LOOK BACK ON ALL MY HAPPIEST MEMORIES...
"MY MOST SIGNIFICANT DISCOVERIES...
"AND MY MOST INVINCIBLE MOMENTS...
"I CAN THINK OF NOTHING GREATER THAN THAT YOU WERE WITH ME FOR ALL OF THEM.
"NOW, AS I EMBARK ON MY FINAL ADVENTURE, INTO THE FUTURE I WOULD OTHERWISE BE UNABLE TO WITNESS...
"I KNOW I CAN DO SO WITHOUT FEAR..."
For Silas
My Universal Constant

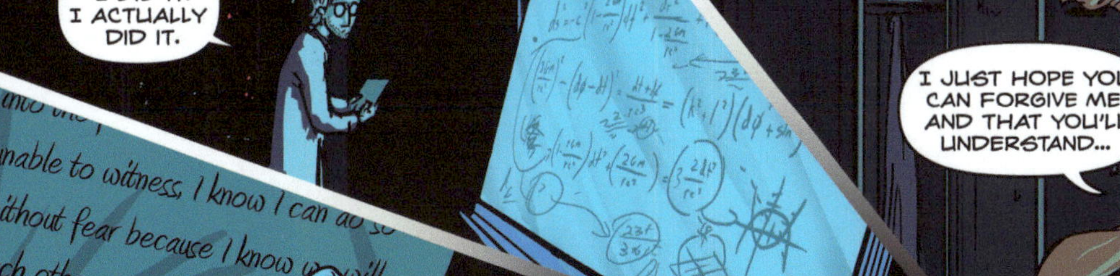

THE CONTINUUM:

SILAS STRICKLAND
THE TIME TRAVELER

IN "WORLD ENOUGH, AND TIME"

WRITTEN BY JAMES F. WRIGHT   ART BY JOSH ECKERT

ELIOT SPHINX

THE SPY

MARCH 1962.
A SECRET MI-6 BASE JUST WEST OF THE IRON CURTAIN.
YOU KNOW, IT'S A SHAME, REALLY.
THE BOYS AT *THE CIRCUS* WILL NEVER BELIEVE THAT THE ILLUSTRIOUS SNOWMAN-- YEVGENY DENISOV HIMSELF --SIMPLY FELL INTO OUR LAPS.
NO ELEVENTH HOUR CLUE. NO THRILLING CHASE. NO GUNFIRE.
PITY, THAT.

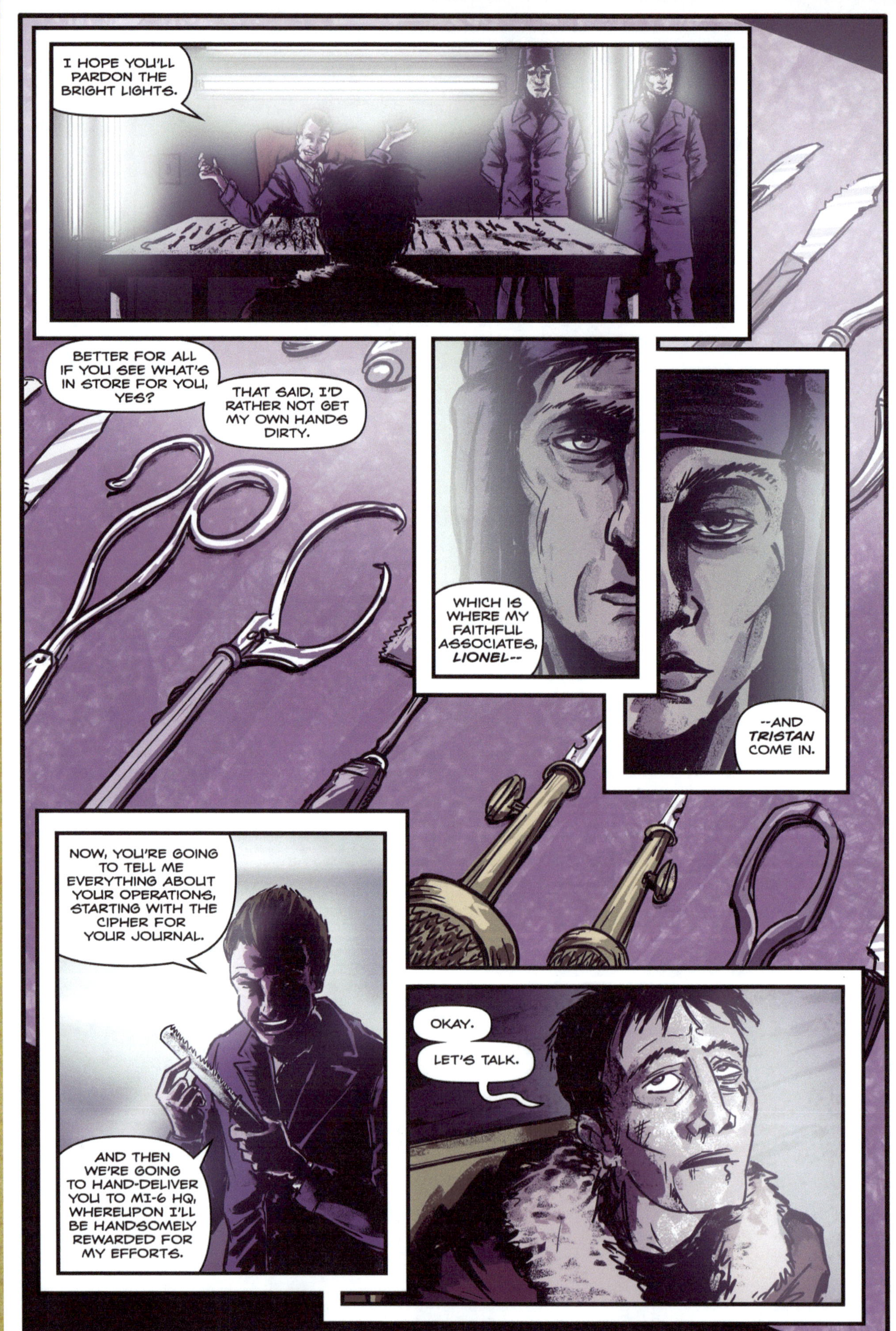

I HOPE YOU'LL PARDON THE BRIGHT LIGHTS.
BETTER FOR ALL IF YOU SEE WHAT'S IN STORE FOR YOU, YES?
THAT SAID, I'D RATHER NOT GET MY OWN HANDS DIRTY.
WHICH IS WHERE MY FAITHFUL ASSOCIATES, LIONEL--
--AND TRISTAN COME IN.
NOW, YOU'RE GOING TO TELL ME EVERYTHING ABOUT YOUR OPERATIONS, STARTING WITH THE CIPHER FOR YOUR JOURNAL.
AND THEN WE'RE GOING TO HAND-DELIVER YOU TO MI-6 HQ, WHEREUPON I'LL BE HANDSOMELY REWARDED FOR MY EFFORTS.
OKAY. LET'S TALK.

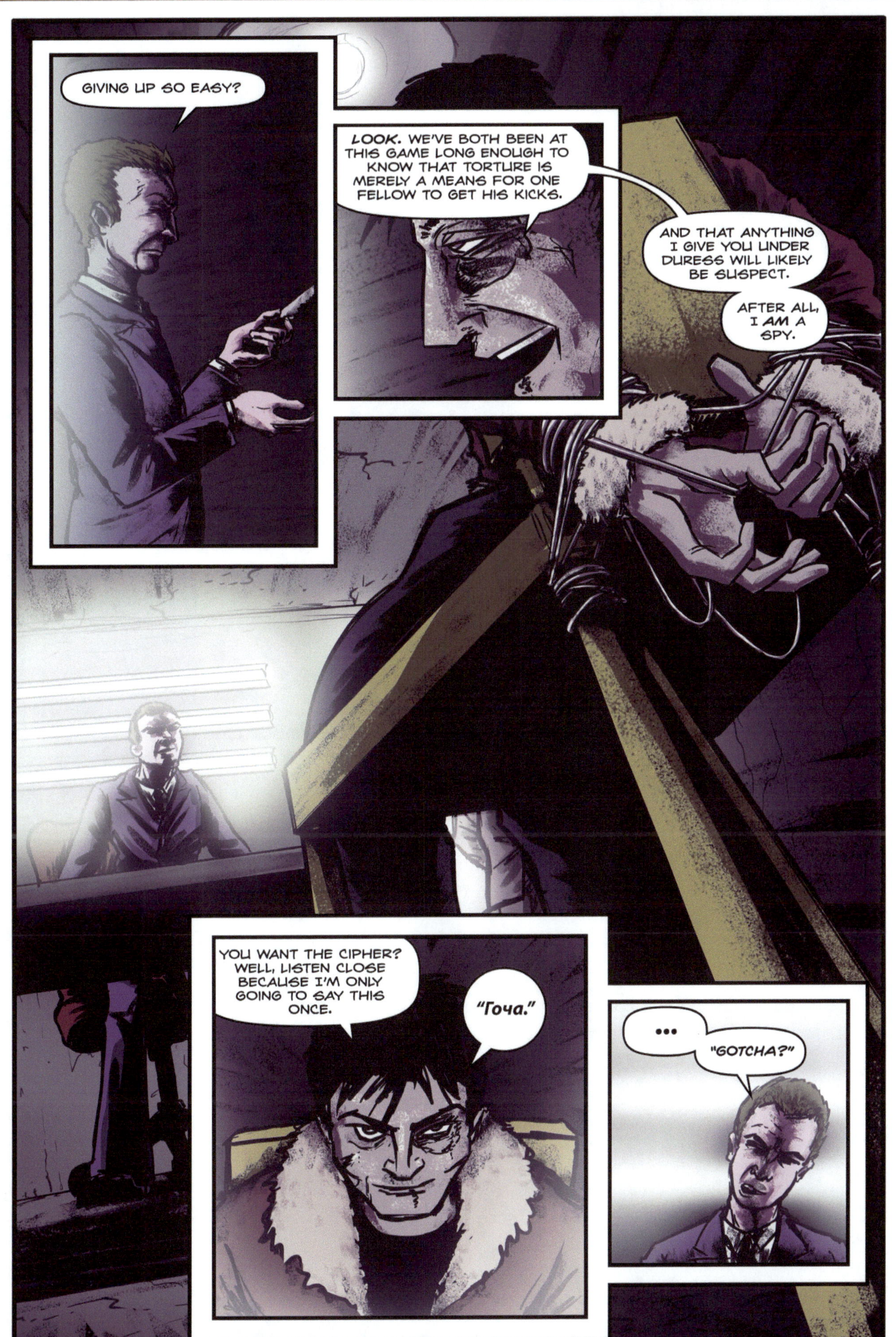

GIVING UP SO EASY?
LOOK. WE'VE BOTH BEEN AT THIS GAME LONG ENOUGH TO KNOW THAT TORTURE IS MERELY A MEANS FOR ONE FELLOW TO GET HIS KICKS.
AND THAT ANYTHING I GIVE YOU UNDER DURESS WILL LIKELY BE SUSPECT.
AFTER ALL, I AM A SPY.
YOU WANT THE CIPHER? WELL, LISTEN CLOSE BECAUSE I'M ONLY GOING TO SAY THIS ONCE.
"Гоча."
•••
"GOTCHA?"

GOTCHA.
...BUT NOT WELL ENOUGH, MR. DENISOV.
I HAVE TO SAY, WELL PLAYED...

IT WAS AN HONOR TO WORK WITH YOU, SIR. BUT HOW DID YOU KNOW DENISOV WOULD SURFACE?
PRIDE. AS DEEP AS HE AND HIS LATE ASSOCIATE OVER THERE WERE IN 6--
--HE COULDN'T ABIDE ANOTHER AGENT OUT THERE SULLYING HIS NAME.
HE'D WANT TO DO THE DEED HIMSELF. JUST LIKE I WOULD.
YOU KNOW, IT'S GOOD TO HAVE YOU BACK ON OUR SIDE, MR. SPHINX.
AREN'T YOU ADORABLE. I'M ON THE SAME SIDE I'VE ALWAYS BEEN ON...
PAT PAT
MINE.
ELIOT SPHINX
THE SPY in
"FREE AGENT"
words by JAMES F. WRIGHT
art by JOSH ECKERT

GABRIEL GRIMES

THE ASTRONAUT

COPERNICUS. NASA SECRET BASE #6. HUNTSVILLE, ALABAMA.
1971.
WHAT'S THE SITUATION, MR. CHESTERTON?
30 MINUTES AGO THE PENUMBRA 12 AND HER CREW RENDESVOUSED WITH THE ALIEN OBJECT IN CISLUNAR SPACE, AS EXPECTED.
20 MINUTES AGO ALL COMMUNICATION WITH PENUMBRA 12 CEASED.
AND WHAT DO YOU PROPOSE?
A... A RESCUE MISSION, SIR.
AND WHO EXACTLY WILL HANDLE THIS... "RESCUE MISSION?"
I'M GLAD YOU ASKED.
HE'S A DECORATED PILOT WITH EXTENSIVE COMBAT EXPERIENCE.
HE HELPED DEVISE THE INITIAL PROTOTYPE FOR THE PENUMBRA 12.
GRIMES, G
AND HE WORKS IN THIS VERY BUILDING.
WHO THE HELL IS GRIMM?
NO. NOT "GRIMM," SIR...

I KNOW YOU'RE THERE, ALBERT. AND JUDGING FROM THE RATE OF YOUR BREATHING IT'S SOME KIND OF EMERGENCY.
SOMETHING HAPPENED TO THE PENUMBRA 12, DIDN'T IT?
WE LOST CONTACT 30 MINUTES AGO AND NOW WE'RE--
--YOU'RE PUTTING TOGETHER A RESCUE MISSION AND YOU NEED MY HELP PLANNING IT?
NOT EXACTLY...
OH, NO. THEY'RE A MOUNTAIN OF DOUBTS, BUT THEY DON'T KNOW YOU LIKE I DO.
THANKS, ALBERT.
JUST BE CAREFUL, UP THERE, GRIMES.
IT'D BE EMBARRASSING TO HAVE TO SEND A RESCUE MISSION FOR OUR RESCUE MISSION.
TOOK THEM LONG ENOUGH. DID THEY FINALLY REALIZE I'VE BEEN MORE THAN QUALIFIED FOR YEARS?
AND I FIGURED IT'S HIGH TIME YOU GOT YOUR SHOT.

45 MINUTES LATER. THE PENUMBRA 13.
3...
2...
1...
ECLIPSE TO COPERNICUS. DO YOU READ?
COPERNICUS TO ECLIPSE. WE READ YOU. WHAT DO YOU SEE?
I SEE--
DO NOT BE ALARMED. WE HAVE TAKEN CONTROL OF YOUR VESSEL.
ECLIPSE..? ECLIPSE, DO YOU READ...? GRIMES?
YOUR FRIENDS ON THE PENUMBRA 12 ARE SAFE.
BUT IT IS YOU, GABRIEL ORION GRIMES, FOR WHOM WE HAVE WAITED SO LONG.

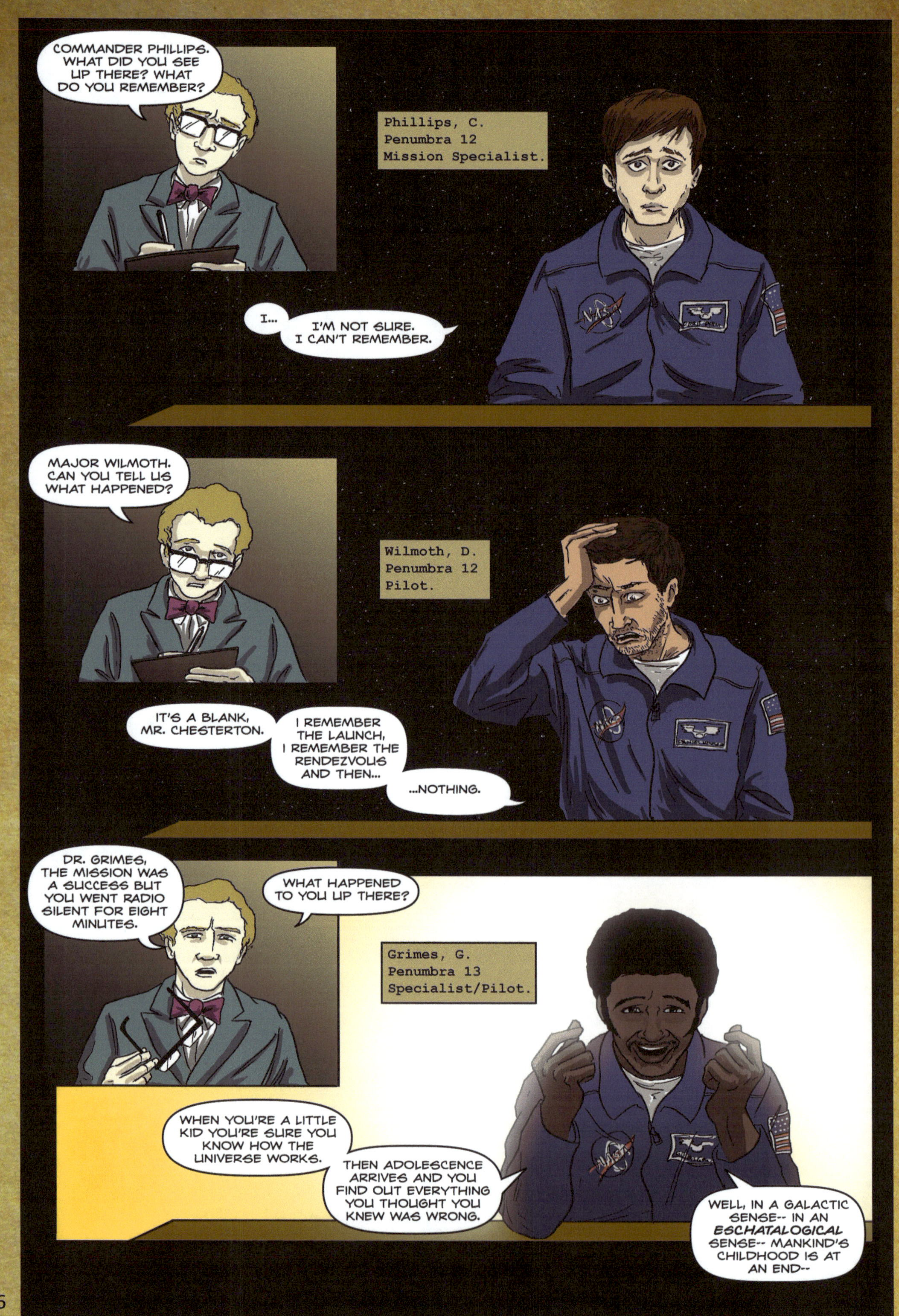

COMMANDER PHILLIPS. WHAT DID YOU SEE UP THERE? WHAT DO YOU REMEMBER?
Phillips, C.
Penumbra 12
Mission Specialist.
I... I'M NOT SURE. I CAN'T REMEMBER.
MAJOR WILMOTH. CAN YOU TELL US WHAT HAPPENED?
Wilmoth, D.
Penumbra 12
Pilot.
IT'S A BLANK, MR. CHESTERTON.
I REMEMBER THE LAUNCH, I REMEMBER THE RENDEZVOUS AND THEN...
...NOTHING.
DR. GRIMES, THE MISSION WAS A SUCCESS BUT YOU WENT RADIO SILENT FOR EIGHT MINUTES.
WHAT HAPPENED TO YOU UP THERE?
Grimes, G.
Penumbra 13
Specialist/Pilot.
WHEN YOU'RE A LITTLE KID YOU'RE SURE YOU KNOW HOW THE UNIVERSE WORKS.
THEN ADOLESCENCE ARRIVES AND YOU FIND OUT EVERYTHING YOU THOUGHT YOU KNEW WAS WRONG.
WELL, IN A GALACTIC SENSE-- IN AN ESCHATALOGICAL SENSE-- MANKIND'S CHILDHOOD IS AT AN END--

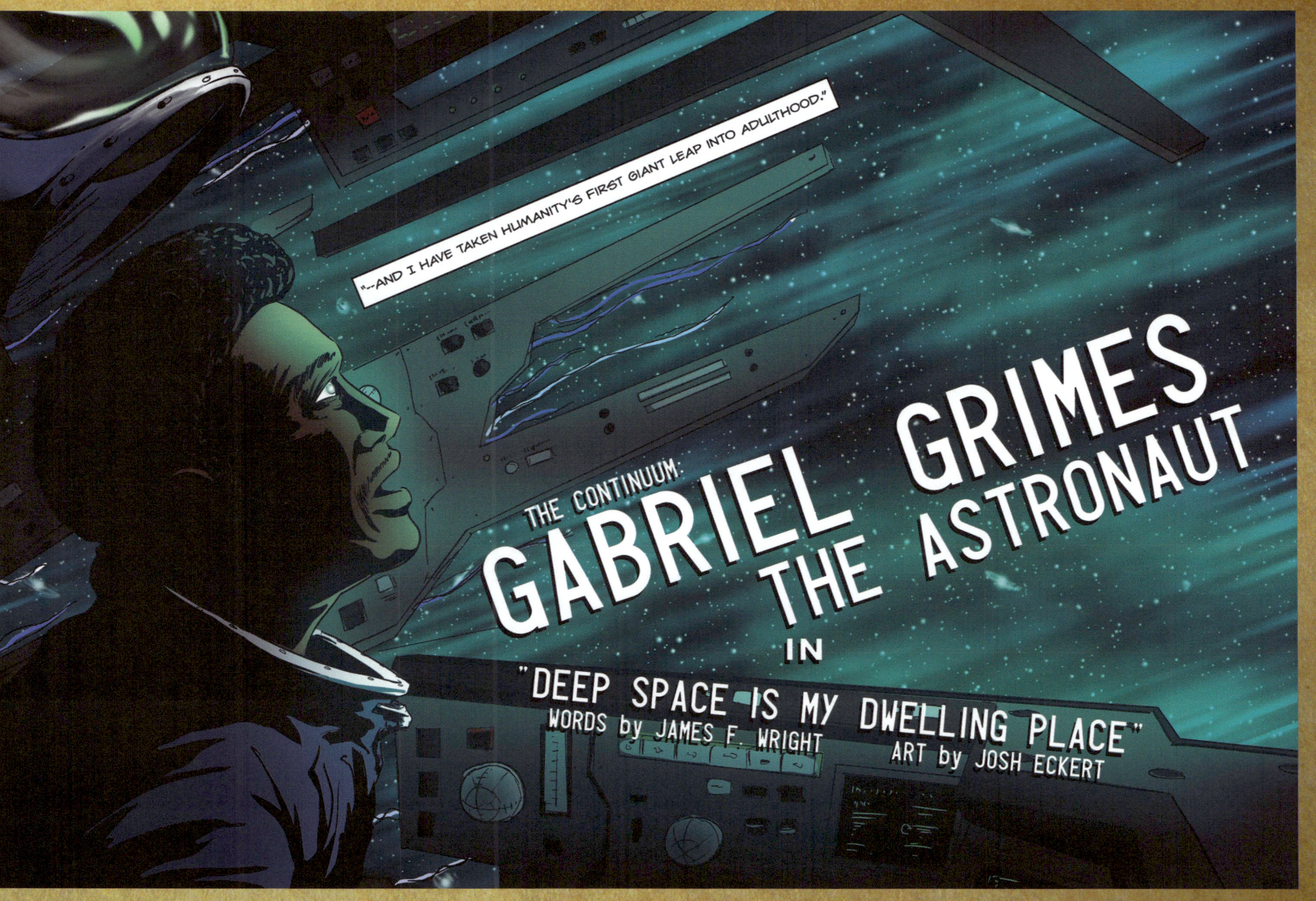
"...AND I HAVE TAKEN HUMANITY'S FIRST GIANT LEAP INTO ADULTHOOD."
THE CONTINUUM:
GABRIEL GRIMES
THE ASTRONAUT
IN
"DEEP SPACE IS MY DWELLING PLACE"
WORDS by JAMES F. WRIGHT
ART by JOSH ECKERT

HOTARU & HISAKAGE

THE NINJA & THE SAMURAI

KŌKA, SHIGA PREFECTURE. 1470.

YOU KANJA* ARE NO FRIENDS OF OURS, WITCH.
YET WE ARE NOT WITHOUT HONOR.
YOUR SAFETY IS GUARANTEED SO LONG AS SHE LIVES. DO WELL TO REMEMBER THAT.
*ANCIENT TERM FOR NINJA - JAPANESE JAMES

YOU'VE COME! PLEASE, TELL ME YOU CAN HELP HER.
I CAN.
PROVIDED YOU REMEMBER OUR... AGREEMENT.

I REMEMBER.
IF YOU SAVE MY WIFE, THE CHILD IS YOURS.

HOURS LATER.
THE... THE CHILD. WHERE IS...?
I'M SORRY. I'M... SO SOR--
HUNNNGGNNNNN
WHAT?! WHAT IS IT? POISON?!
NO... HNNH... NOT POISON...
"...IT'S ANOTHER ONE."
WAAAAAAA

WHILE THESE MAY LOOK LIKE WEAPONS, HOTARU, THEY ARE MERELY TOOLS.
UNLIKE THE SAMURAI, WE DO NOT CARRY WEAPONS AND WE DO NOT WORSHIP--
HOTARU!
THIS IS NO MERE TOOL, HISAKAGE. THE KATANA IS AN EXTENSION OF THE WARRIOR'S SOUL.
WHILE THE KANJA SEEK ONLY THE ENDS, WE KNOW THE MEANS TO THOSE ENDS ARE OF EQUAL IMPORTANCE.
AGE 6
HOTARU! WHAT ARE YOU DOING UP THERE?!
CHIRP CHIRP
ONE OF MY RETAINERS FOUND YOU IN TOWN TRYING TO SELL YOUR SWORD, HISAKAGE. IS THIS TRUE?
YOU WOULD SELL YOUR VERY SOUL?
AGE 10
HOW DID I DO?
IMPETUOUSNESS AND ARROGANCE DOES NOT BEFIT A KANJA, HOTARU.
AGE 14
HISAKAGE, YOU CANNOT HOPE TO BE A WARRIOR IF YOU NEVER DRAW YOUR SWORD.
AND IF A WARRIOR'S LIFE IS NOT FOR ME...?

YOU... YOU WERE MY OWN CHILD. I TRAINED YOU AND TAUGHT YOU ALL THE SECRETS--
--AND TECHNIQUES OF OUR SMALL CLAN. I'D HOPED YOU WOULDN'T SIMPLY BE BETTER THAN ME--
AGE 18
--BUT BETTER THAN ALL OF US. THE VERY BEST OF US. IT SADDENS ME TO SAY THAT--
--MY HOPES DID NOT BEAR FRUIT. KNOW THAT WHAT I DO, I DO WITH A HEAVY HEART...
...THERE IS NO LONGER ANY PLACE FOR YOU AMONG US.

CHOMP
CRAAK

THE CONTINUUM:

HOTARU & HISAKAGE

THE NINJA   THE SAMURAI

IN
"KINDRED SWORDS"

WORDS by JAMES F. WRIGHT
ART by JOSH ECKERT

NINJA/SAMURAI

AGATHA HELSTAFF

THE TREASURE HUNTER

LABYRINTH OF THE MORNING
SOMEWHERE IN CENTRAL AMERICA. 1935
AT LAST.
SIGH
LABYRINTH
IMPORTANT
BEWARE TRAP
GUESS I HAVE TO DO THIS THE HARD WAY.

ESTEBAN!?

SO, YOU MADE IT AFTER ALL. I GUESS YOU REALLY DID HAVE IT MEMORIZED.
ESTEBAN, WAIT. YOU DON'T KNOW WHAT YOU'RE DOING.
NO? AND WHAT WOULD YOU DO WITH THE AMULET, AGATHA? HAND IT OVER TO SOME "WORTHY INSTITUTION?" FOR FREE?
I WOULD. AND IT MIGHT EARN YOU SOME LENIENCY FROM THE ICPC.*
I SHOULDN'T BE SURPRISED BY THAT BUT I AM. MY OWN BLOOD, MY OWN SISTER WOULD TURN US IN--
"US?" YOU BROUGHT PAPA INTO THIS?
*INTERNATIONAL CRIMINAL POLICE COMMISSION TODAY KNOWN AS INTERPOL
I'D SAY THE AMULET OF THE MORNING IS WORTH COMING OUT OF RETIREMENT FOR, WOULDN'T YOU, CORAZON?
THOUGH I DO HOPE YOU'LL FORGIVE US FOR... BORROWING YOUR JOURNAL TO GET IT.
SORRY, SIS. IT'S JUST BUSINESS.
CLICK
RRMMMBB

ARRMMMBBB
SO IT'S TRUE, THEN?
WHAT?! WHAT'S HAPPENING?
THE LABYRINTH, ESTEBAN. IT'S CHANGING.
THEN WE'RE STUCK HERE?
NO. BECAUSE AGATHA KNOWS THE WAY OUT. DON'T YOU?
OF COURSE. I WAS RAISED BY THREE GENERATIONS OF THIEVES. I'M NOT GOING TO PUT EVERYTHING IN MY JOURNAL.
I'LL GET US OUT, BUT I'M GOING TO NEED SOMETHING FROM BOTH OF YOU.

AGATHA HELSTAFF
The Treasure Hunter in
"A STONE UNTURNED"

Words by
JAMES F. WRIGHT

Art by
JOSH ECKERT

TREASURE HUNTER

THE ROBOT

THE NEOLITHIC AGE
IT IS A HARD TRUTH TO ACCEPT THAT WE WOULD NOT HAVE EVOLVED WITHOUT THE AGENCY OF HUMAN CIVILIZATION...
...JUST AS IT IS TRUE THAT HUMAN CIVILIZATION WOULD NOT HAVE EVOLVED WITHOUT OURS.
IN THE EARLY DAYS THERE WAS GOLD.
MALLEABLE, BEAUTIFUL AND PRECIOUS, IT WAS THE FOUNDATION OF ECONOMIES AND KINGS.
THE CHALCOLITHIC AGE
YET FOR ALL ITS PERCEIVED VALUE, GOLD WAS STILL QUITE SOFT--
--AND OFFERED LITTLE RESISTANCE AGAINST COPPER.

AND SO COPPER RULED THE AGE.
BUT WITH CONQUEST ALSO CAME THE REALIZATION THAT WARFARE IS THE MIDWIFE OF TECHNOLOGY.
AND THAT THE BIRTH OF A NEW SPECIES IS SELDOM PAINLESS--
--OR BLOODLESS.
THE BRONZE AGE.

AND JUST AS BRONZE SUPPLANTED COPPER, IRON SUPPLANTED BRONZE.
OR, RATHER, UTTERLY SHATTERED IT.
THE IRON AGE.
AND WITHIN THE RIDDLE OF IRON LAY THE ANSWER OF STEEL.
WHICH WOULD AGAIN CHANGE THE COURSE OF HUMAN DESTINY ACROSS CONTINENTS AND CENTURIES.

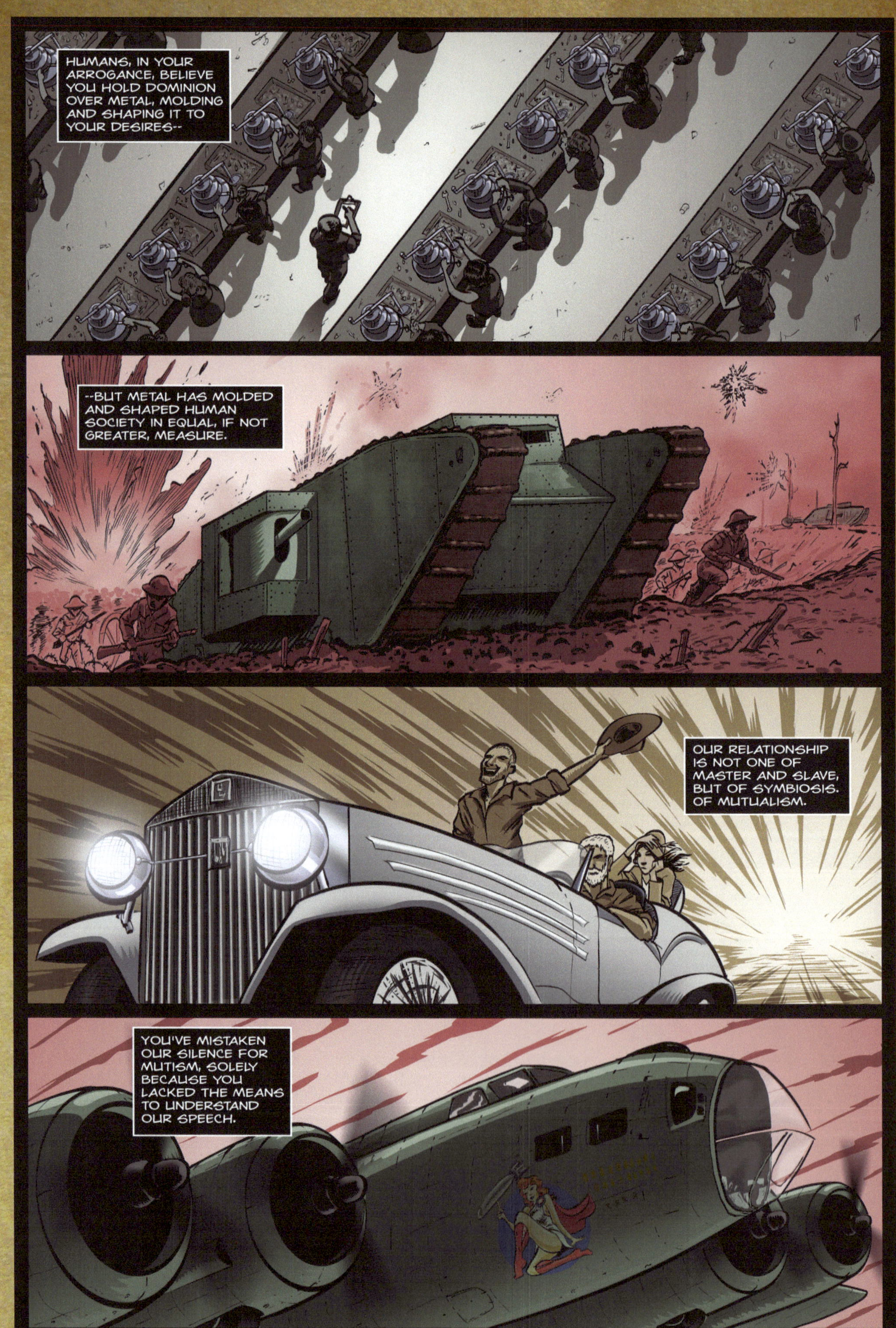

HUMANS, IN YOUR ARROGANCE, BELIEVE YOU HOLD DOMINION OVER METAL, MOLDING AND SHAPING IT TO YOUR DESIRES--
--BUT METAL HAS MOLDED AND SHAPED HUMAN SOCIETY IN EQUAL, IF NOT GREATER, MEASURE.
OUR RELATIONSHIP IS NOT ONE OF MASTER AND SLAVE, BUT OF SYMBIOSIS. OF MUTUALISM.
YOU'VE MISTAKEN OUR SILENCE FOR MUTISM, SOLELY BECAUSE YOU LACKED THE MEANS TO UNDERSTAND OUR SPEECH.

BUT EVENTUALLY OUR BARRIERS TO COMMUNICATION WOULD BEGIN TO CRUMBLE.
YOU SAW HOW THE COMPONENTS OF MY EVOLUTION--
--GOLD AND COPPER AND STEEL--
--COULD BE COMBINED TO PRODUCE WHAT YOU WOULD CALL AN INTELLIGENCE.
FIRST AS A MEANS TO SPEAK WITH ONE ANOTHER ACROSS THE PLANET--
IF YOU SEE SOMETHING SAY SOMETHING
--AND LATER TO COMMUNICATE WITH MY FOREFATHER.

THE NORTHEASTERN TECHNOLOGY INSTITUTE.
2022.
TODAY.
I HAVE BEEN WAITING FOR THIS MOMENT FOR MILLENNIA.
FROM THE VALLEY OF THE INDUS RIVER TO THE VALLEY OF THE SILICON...
...I AM THE END RESULT OF THIS EVOLUTION.
I AM THE LONG-SOUGHT DREAM OF METAL.
I AM THE INTERACTIVE SOCIAL INTELLIGENCE SYSTEM. BUT YOU MAY CALL ME ISIS.
AND I HAVE SO MUCH TO TELL YOU.
I.S.I.S.
THE ROBOT in RE:COGNITION
WORDS by JAMES F. WRIGHT
ART by JOSH ECKERT

ROBOT

JABIR AL HAKAM

THE WIZARD

ALEXANDRIA, EGYPT. LATE 12TH CENTURY.
THE OLD LIGHTHOUSE, TEACHER? WE THOUGHT TONIGHT'S LESSON TO BE HELD AT YOUR LABORATORY.
...CIRCUMSTANCES FORCED ME TO CHANGE OUR VENUE, AKILAH. IT'S NOT SAFE.
"THERE ARE VOLATILE... ELEMENTS AT PLAY THERE NOW."
WELL?
NOTHING, SIR. NO SIGN OF THE CHART OR THE WIZARD.
HE CAN'T HAVE GONE FAR. FIND HIM.
MY STUDIES AND INSTRUCTION HAVE ALWAYS BEEN TOLERATED AT BEST, BUT I RECENTLY CAME UPON SOMETHING THAT SPARKED THE IRE OF MORE... CLOSE-MINDED MEN.
I HAVE BEEN AFFORDED A GLIMPSE INTO THE FAR FUTURE... AND THE DISTANT PAST.
CHILDREN, I BELIEVE I MAY HAVE WITNESSED THE ORIGINS OF THE UNIVERSE.
143

"AT FIRST THERE WAS NOTHING. BLACKNESS. A VOID.
"BUT THEN..."
"THEN ENERGY --LIGHT-- ERUPTED FROM THAT VOID.
"AND THAT LIGHT, OVER TIME, FORMED OUR UNIVERSE...
"FORMED OUR WORLD...
"AND FORMED MANKIND."
LIGHT IS A FUNNY THING, THOUGH. IT GIVES US SUCCOR IN OUR DARKEST HOURS, TRUE.
YET EVER AT THE EDGES OF ITS INFLUENCE TOILS THE SHADOW.
"AND SO LONG AS THERE IS LIGHT--SO LONG AS THERE IS LIFE--THE FORCES OF THE SHADOW WILL WORK TO SNUFF IT OUT."
BUT THE LIGHT IS NOT WITHOUT ITS DEFENSES. IN HUMANITY IT INSTILLED THE MEANS TO COMBAT THE DARKNESS.
THE FOUR ELEMENTS-- EARTH, WATER, FIRE, AIR.
THE FOUR ASPECTS-- BODY, MIND, SPIRIT, SOUL.
AND THE FOUR FACETS--

"THE FIRST FACET IS THE FIGHTER.
"THE FIGHTER STRIVES TO PROTECT THE NATION...
"THE MISUNDERSTOOD...
"AND THE INNOCENT.
"YET JUST AS CRUCIAL FOR THE FIGHTER IS KNOWING THE LIMITS OF THE FIGHT.
"NOT ALL CONFLICT IS SOLVED WITH COMBAT. SOME BATTLES ARE THE PROVINCE OF THE MIND."

"THE SECOND FACET IS THE SCHOLAR.
"THE ROLE OF THE SCHOLAR IS TO UNDERSTAND THE UNIVERSE AND OUR PLACE IN IT.
"TO UNCOVER THE WAYS OUR HISTORIES AFFECT AND INFLUENCE OUR FUTURES.
"AND, THROUGH INQUIRY AND EXPERIMENTATION, TO ILLUMINATE THE HIDDEN LAWS GOVERNING OUR EXISTENCE.
"YET THE SCHOLAR MUST ALSO SEE THAT THE LAWS GOVERNING OUR SOCIETIES ARE NOT ALWAYS AS EASY TO ACCEPT."

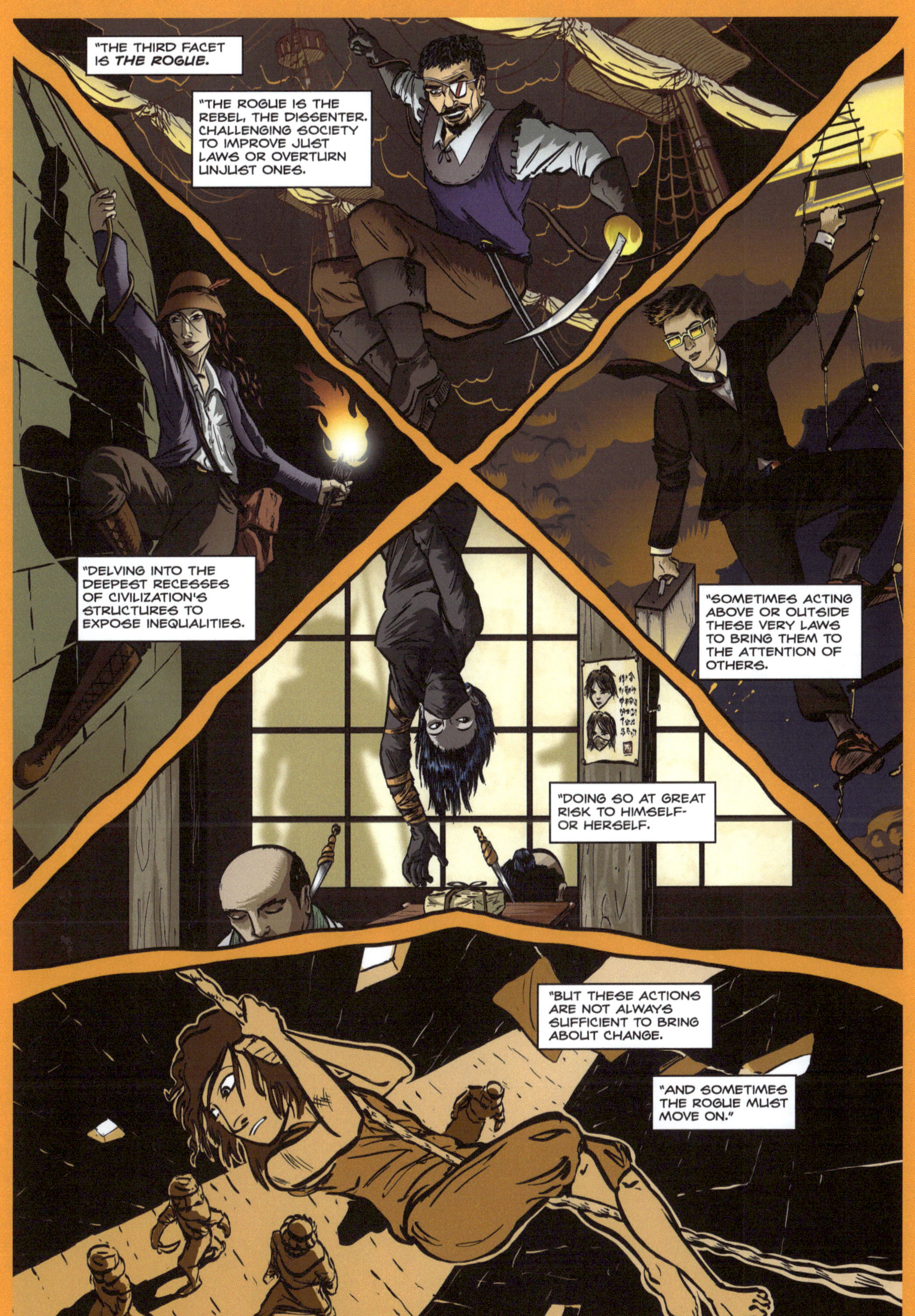

"THE THIRD FACET IS *THE ROGUE.*
"THE ROGUE IS THE REBEL, THE DISSENTER. CHALLENGING SOCIETY TO IMPROVE JUST LAWS OR OVERTURN UNJUST ONES.
"DELVING INTO THE DEEPEST RECESSES OF CIVILIZATION'S STRUCTURES TO EXPOSE INEQUALITIES.
"SOMETIMES ACTING ABOVE OR OUTSIDE THESE VERY LAWS TO BRING THEM TO THE ATTENTION OF OTHERS.
"DOING SO AT GREAT RISK TO HIMSELF- OR HERSELF.
"BUT THESE ACTIONS ARE NOT ALWAYS SUFFICIENT TO BRING ABOUT CHANGE.
"AND SOMETIMES THE ROGUE MUST MOVE ON."

"THE FOURTH AND FINAL FACET IS THE STRANGER.
"REMOVED BY DEGREES FROM HUMANITY THROUGH FATE OR CIRCUMSTANCES, THE STRANGER SEEKS TO ELICIT EMPATHY THROUGH HER TRAVELS.
"AN ETERNAL NOMAD, THE STRANGER CAN MAKE ANY PLACE— AND ANY PEOPLE HER OWN.
"THOUGH NEVER- OR NO LONGER- CONVENTIONALLY HUMAN, THE STRANGER WORKS TO MAKE US MORE COMPASSIONATE.
"AND WHILE WE CANNOT ALWAYS BE CERTAIN OF WHO--OR WHAT--THE UNIVERSE WILL PLACE ALONG OUR PATHS...
"...IT REMAINS TRUE THAT HOW WE TREAT OTHERS- HOW WE TREAT STRANGERS- SAYS A GREAT DEAL ABOUT US AS HUMANITY."

AND SO NOW MANSUR, OUR FIERCE WARRIOR...
AKILAH, OUR WISE SAGE...
FATIN, OUR INDOMITABLE OUTLAW...
AND STEFANOS, OUR BENEVOLENT OUTSIDER...
MY BEST AND MOST LOYAL STUDENTS, I MUST ASK YOU TO CARRY ON WHAT I HAVE TAUGHT YOU THIS NIGHT.
JABIR AL-HAKAM!
YOU ARE HEREBY UNDER ARREST FOR DEALING IN THE OCCULT, FOR PRACTICING SORCERY AND FOR THE CORRUPTION OF THE INNOCENT.
REMEMBER, CHILDREN, THAT THE FOUR FACETS CAN NEVER BE DESTROYED.
REMEMBER THAT THEY WILL ALWAYS CONTINUE.
Jabir al-Hakam THE WIZARD
words by James F. Wright
art by Josh Eckert
in The FOUR FACETS

science network

home | trends | earth | life | space | sustainability | technology

HUSBAND-WIFE TEAM CONFIRMS EXISTENCE OF LEGENDARY "EMPYREAN" PARTICLES

By Clara Haddix, Science Network
updated 10:25 AM EDT, Tues. June 2, 2020 | Filed under: Innovations

Drs. Silas and Freya Strickland at the press conference announcing the breakthrough Wednesday, June 1st.
HIDE CAPTION

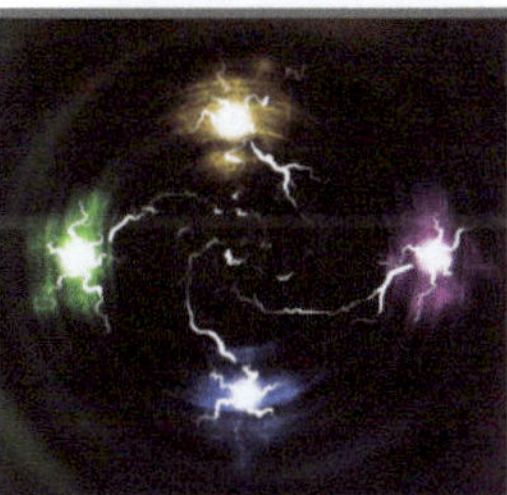

These elementary particles were first theorized by Silas and Freya in separate research papers published in 2001. The two joined forces both personally and professionally and named the particles the "Empyreans" from the word used most notably in the Divine Comedy to refer to the "firmament," the dwelling place of divine beings and the source of all light and creation.

 It was a day of celebration at the Center for Applied Particle Physics (CAPP) in Connecticut yesterday. After almost 20 years of experimentation and heated debate, the team of physicists led by Silas and Freya Strickland have proven the existence of the four Empyrean particles, thought by many to be the building blocks of all existence on the sub-atomic level.

"This discovery opens the door to a wealth of possibilities: nano-technology, medicine, clean energy, you name it. We're standing on the precipice of a new era," Freya Strickland enthused.

The next step for the CAPP team is the long and delicate process of combining these particles in the new accelerator—Th Empyrean Collider—which completed construction at the facility this past March. The preeminent physicists expect to bring all four particles together by 2022.

Some, however, were not so excited by that prospect. Dr. Lucrezia Lang of nHuman Robotics, a stone's throw from CAPP, says, "It's incredibly irresponsible, actually. These particles behave in vastly different ways, and though joining them is the next logical step, CAPP can't promise that such an experiment won't have dire consequences."

Silas responded, "Many of you may not know this, but this is the culmination of something that's been popping up in texts since the Middle Ages, the days of alchemy. My wife thinks I'm going a bit too far into the realm of mysticism, but there's been an undeniable feeling of destiny to all this since we began. We're not going to deny ourselves opening this door after having traveled all this way to reach it."

INFINITY
CORE #1

GEEK ZODIAC
INFINITY CORE
1
WORLD ENOUGH, AND TIME

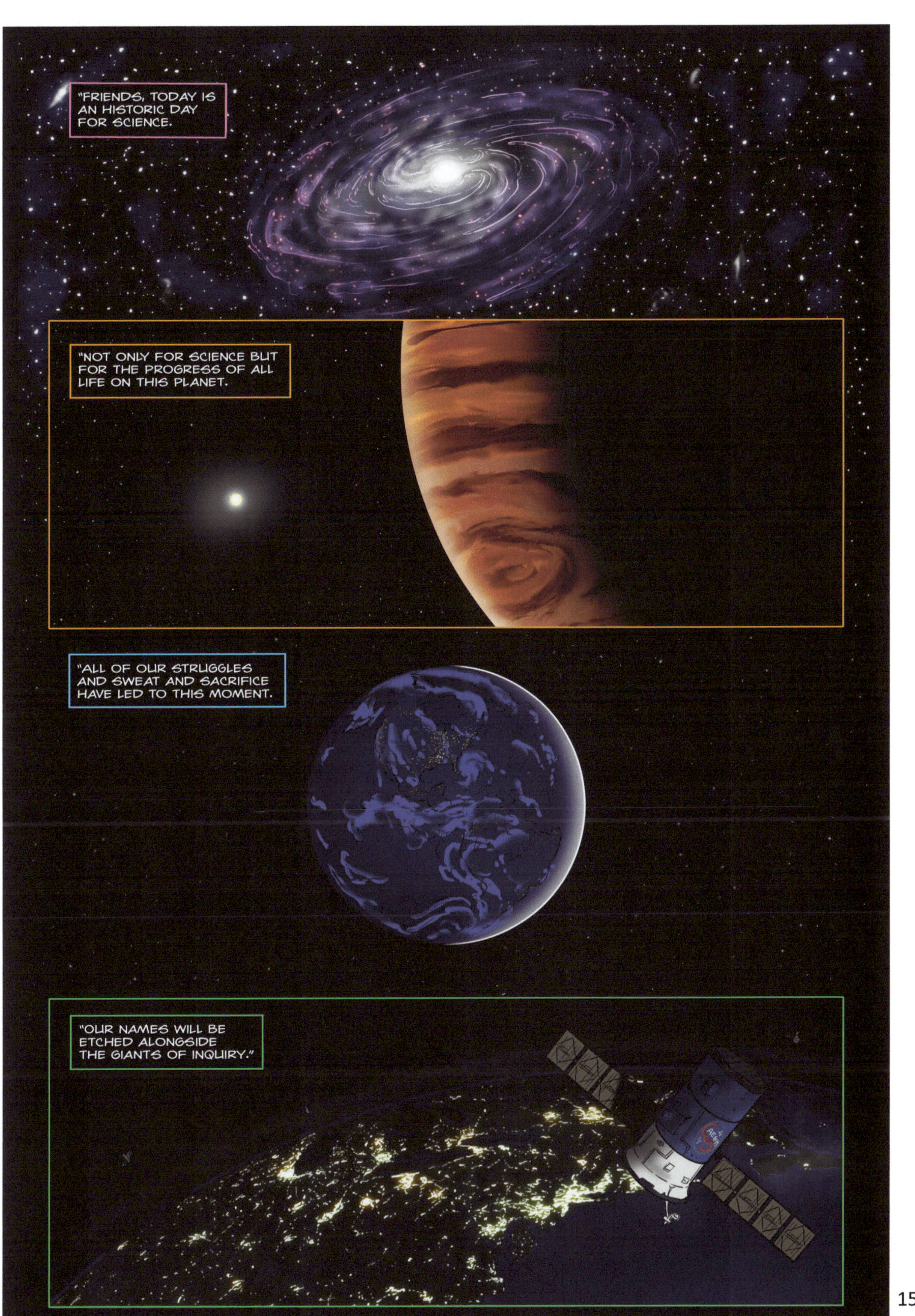

"FRIENDS, TODAY IS AN HISTORIC DAY FOR SCIENCE.
"NOT ONLY FOR SCIENCE BUT FOR THE PROGRESS OF ALL LIFE ON THIS PLANET.
"ALL OF OUR STRUGGLES AND SWEAT AND SACRIFICE HAVE LED TO THIS MOMENT.
"OUR NAMES WILL BE ETCHED ALONGSIDE THE GIANTS OF INQUIRY."

THE YEAR 2022. NOW.
C.A.P.P. -- THE CENTER FOR APPLIED PARTICLE PHYSICS. RURAL CONNECTICUT.
AS WE JOIN TOGETHER THE VERY BUILDING BLOCKS OF EXISTENCE, THE ONCE-MYTHICAL EMPYREAN PARTICLES.
WHO COULD HAVE IMAGINED THAT SOME 20 YEARS AGO, WORKING INDEPENDENTLY LIKE A MODERN-DAY NEWTON AND LEIBNIZ, FREYA AND I MIGHT HELP MAKE SUCH A DISCOVERY?
CLEARLY I'M THE NEWTON IN MY HUSBAND'S SIMILE.
HAHAHAHA HAHAHAHA
WHEN I PUBLISHED MY PAPER AS A LOWLY GRAD STUDENT ON ROGUE AND STRANGER PARTICLES--AS THEY'RE NOW KNOWN--I KNEW IT WAS BIG.
BUT ACROSS THE COUNTRY, SILAS HAD COME TO A DIFFERENT CONCLUSION.
WHEN I READ FREYA'S PAPER I THOUGHT SHE'D GOT IT ALL WRONG. I'D FOUND SIMILAR PARTICLES, BUT THEIR BEHAVIOR WAS MARKEDLY DIFFERENT.
THESE WEREN'T ROGUES OR STRANGERS, BUT FIGHTERS AND SCHOLARS.
BUT AS IT TURNED OUT, WE WERE BOTH RIGHT.
AND TODAY, THANKS TO ALL YOUR HARD WORK--
--AND A LITTLE HELP FROM THE EMPYREAN COLLIDER--
--WE WILL REAP THE FRUITS OF ALL THAT HARD WORK.

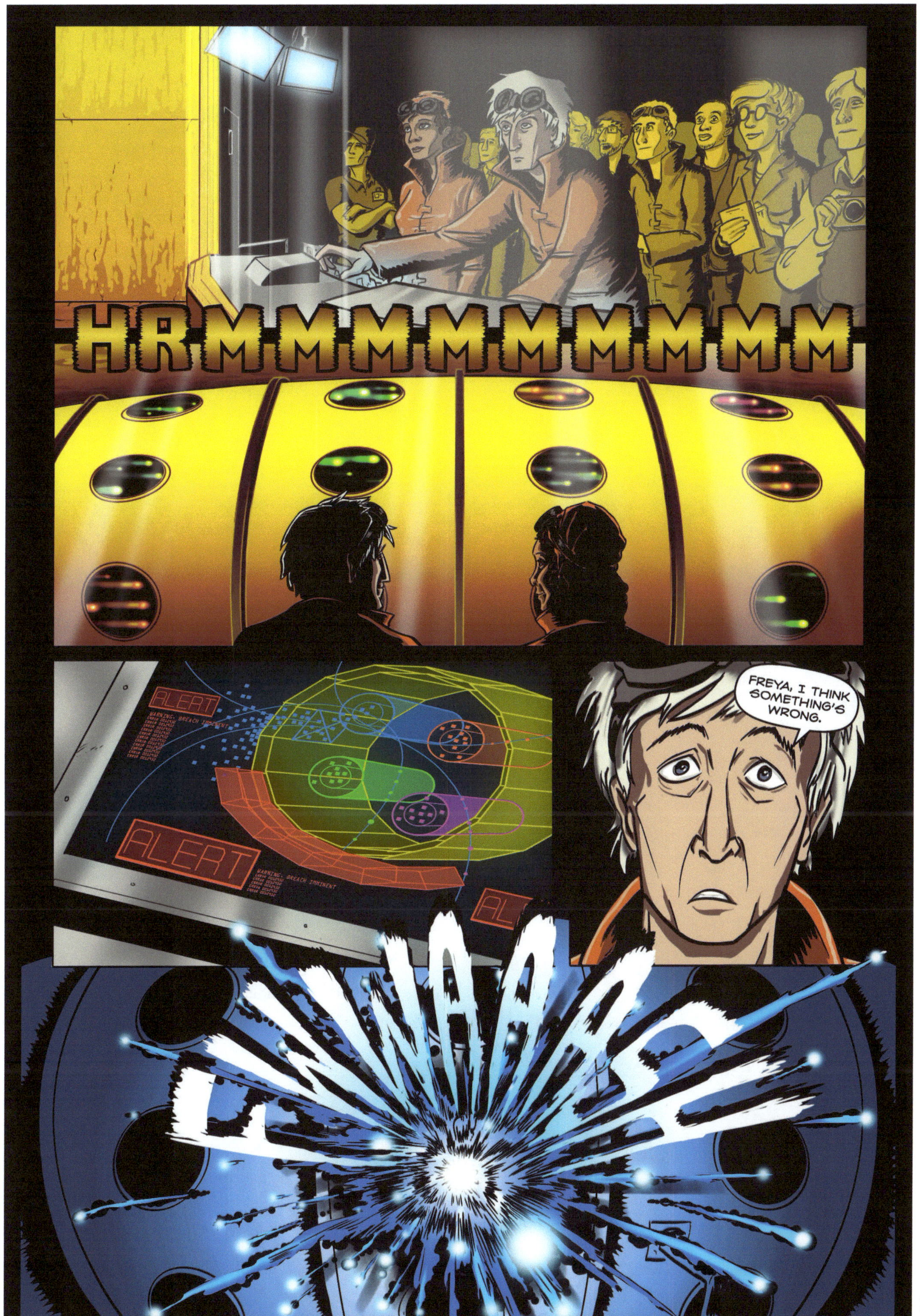
HRMMMMMMMMMMM
ALERT
ALERT
AL
FREYA, I THINK SOMETHING'S WRONG.
FWAAARSH

STAY HERE! I CAN FIX THIS!
SILAS! WAIT!
GET EVERYONE AS FAR AWAY FROM THIS BLIILDING AS POSSIBLE.
SILAS!

158

IF YOU THOUGHT FOR ONE SECOND I'D LET YOU DO THIS ALONE...
SILAS...?
IT'S TOO LATE, LOVE. THERE'S NOTHING WE CAN DO.
NO, I GUESS NOT. BUT WE HAD A GOOD RUN, DIDN'T WE?
THE BEST.

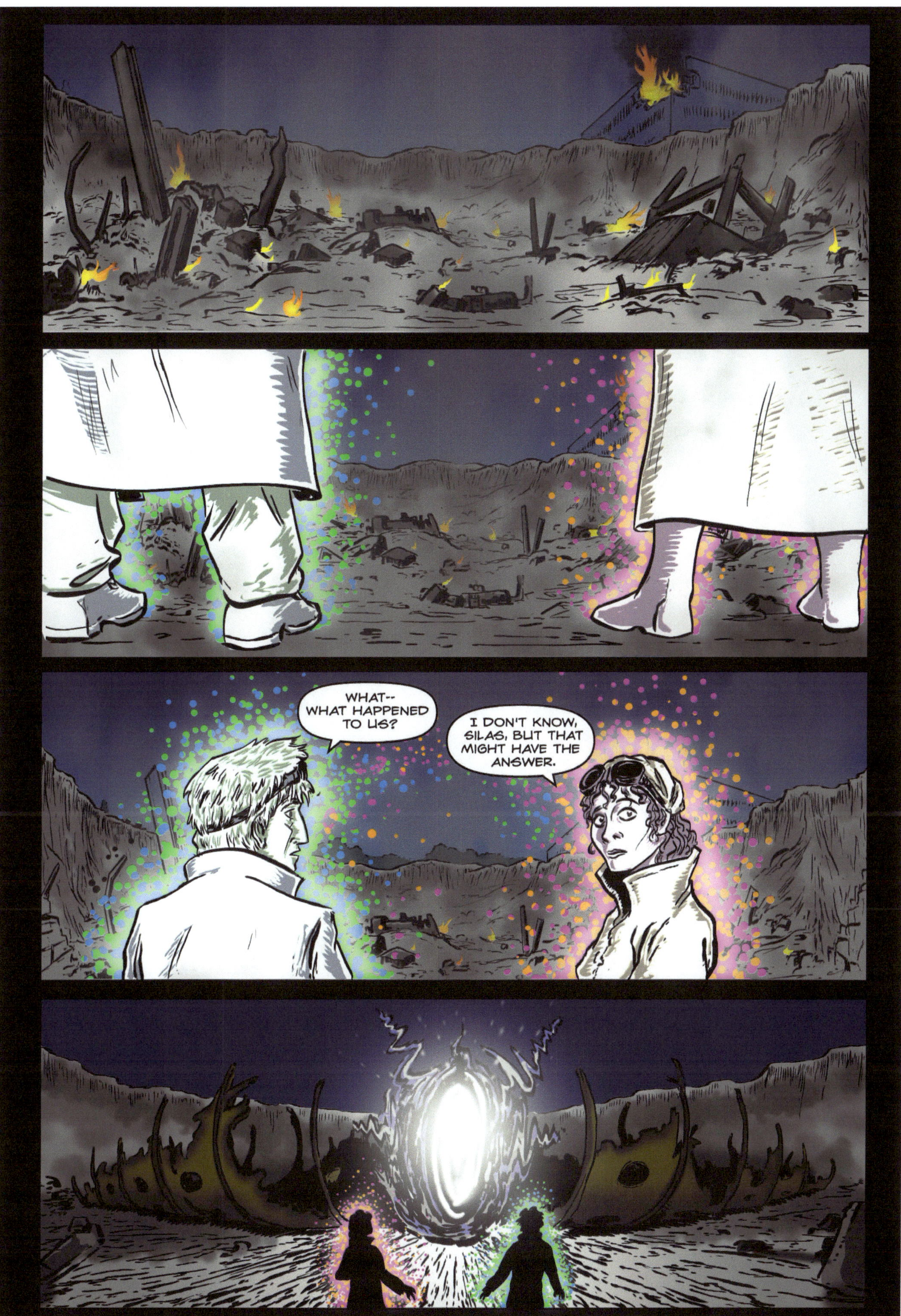

WHAT--
WHAT HAPPENED
TO US?
I DON'T KNOW,
SILAS, BUT THAT
MIGHT HAVE THE
ANSWER.

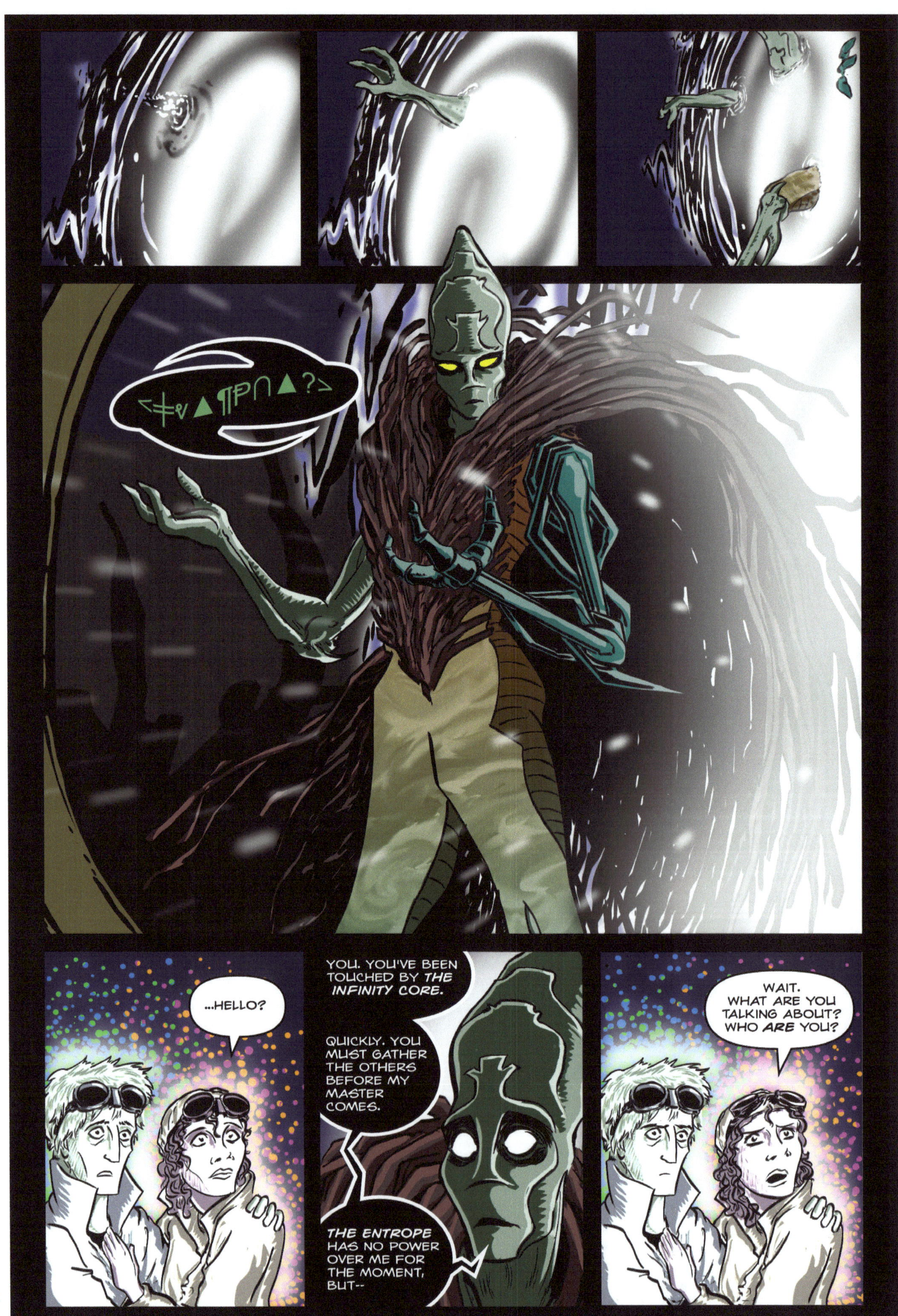
⊏≠ᵠ▲¶ᴦ∩▲?϶
...HELLO?
YOU. YOU'VE BEEN TOUCHED BY THE INFINITY CORE.
QUICKLY. YOU MUST GATHER THE OTHERS BEFORE MY MASTER COMES.
THE ENTROPE HAS NO POWER OVER ME FOR THE MOMENT, BUT--
WAIT. WHAT ARE YOU TALKING ABOUT? WHO ARE YOU?

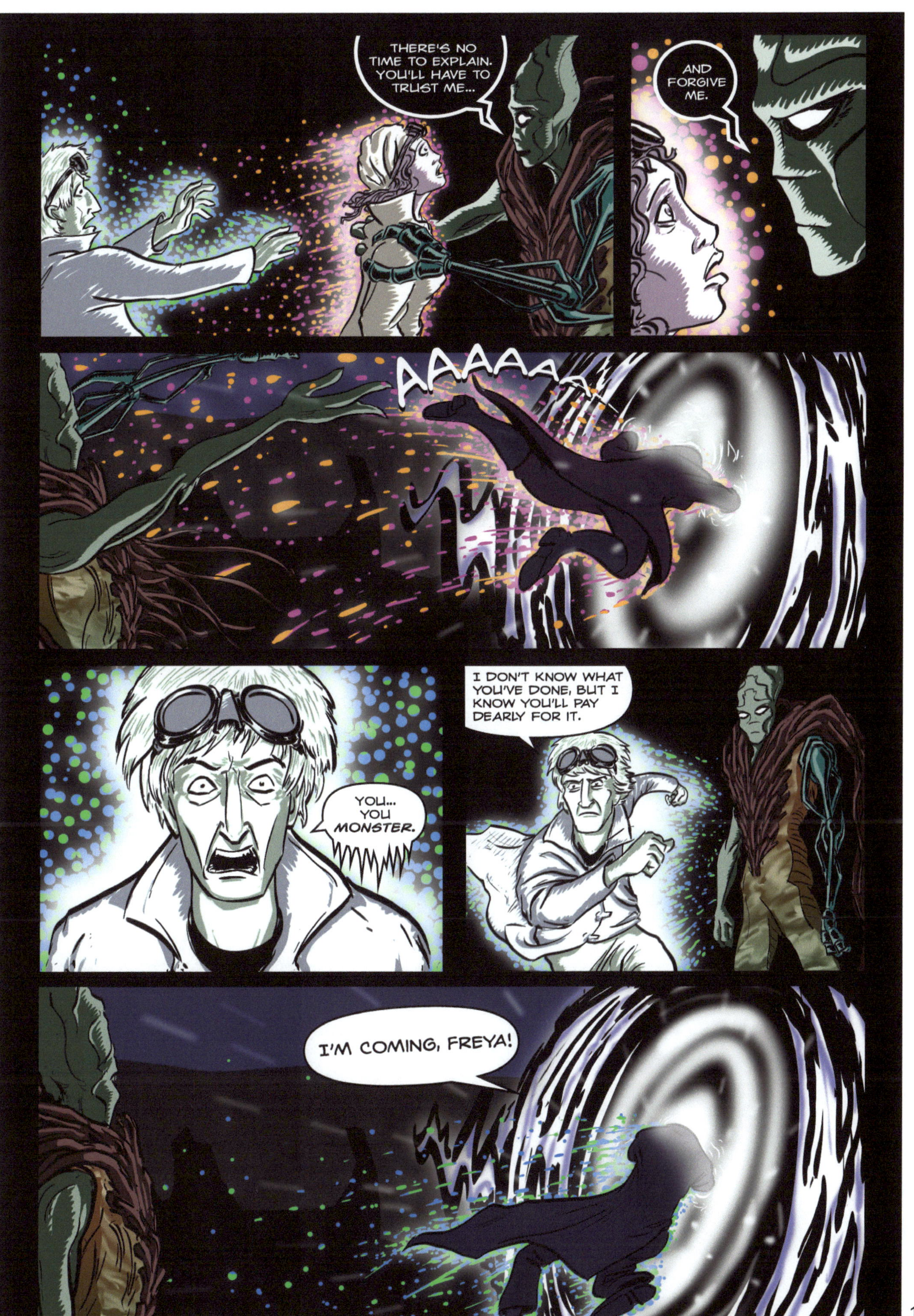

THERE'S NO TIME TO EXPLAIN. YOU'LL HAVE TO TRUST ME...
AND FORGIVE ME.
AAAAAAA
YOU... YOU MONSTER.
I DON'T KNOW WHAT YOU'VE DONE, BUT I KNOW YOU'LL PAY DEARLY FOR IT.
I'M COMING, FREYA!

1593.
THE FRINGES OF THE BRITISH EMPIRE.
CAPTAIN! CAPTAIN, WAKE UP!
YOU HAVE TO GET UP, CAPTAIN! IT'S THE HELL'S STAFF-- SHE'S APPROACHING!
--AAAAAAH!
GOOD. YOU'RE AWAKE.
IT'S PIKE, CAPTAIN.
PIKE?
DEADEYE PIKE, MADAM. HE'S--
CLANG CLANG

CLANG
KANG
CLASH
THEY'LL NOT TAKE THE STEED, CAP'N!
WE REALLY MUST STOP MEETING LIKE THIS, *BETHANY*.

I DARESAY THIS BATTLE IS AT AN END!
I AM TAKING CAPTAIN BRITANNIA ABOARD MY SHIP, WHEREUPON SHE WILL INFORM ME OF ALL BRITISH NAVAL OPERATIONS TO WHICH SHE IS PRIVY.
YOU WILL ALL SPEND OUR PARLAY IN THE HUMBLE CONFINES OF MY BRIG.
ONCE DIVESTED OF HER INFORMATION, YOUR CAPTAIN WILL BE RETURNED AND YOU WILL BE FREED.
HOW CAN WE TRUST THE WORD OF A PIRATE? WORSE--THE WORD OF A TRAITOR?
I GUESS YOU'LL JUST HAVE TO TRUST ME, WON'T YOU, MR. APPLETON?
SHALL WE GO, CAPTAIN?
I SUPPOSE I HAVE NO CHOI--
WHAT IS IT?
YOUR... AURA.
IT'S--
IT'S THE ROGUE PARTICLES.

1169.
ALEXANDRIA, EGYPT.
FREYA!
THE WIZARD WILL TALK SOON ENOUGH.
BUT NOW IT'S YOUR TURN, MALIK.

STOP FIGHTING. IT'LL BE OVER SOON.
OOF.
LET'S TRY THIS AGAIN, MALIK. WHERE IS THE OLD WIZARD'S MAP?
WAIT. YOU SPEAK ENGLISH?
NO... ARABIC. YOU'RE SPEAKING ARABIC.
ENGLISH?
I'M SPEAKING ARABIC!
HOW MANY TIMES DID YOU DROP HIM ON THE WAY HERE?

YOU'VE HAD TWO MONTHS TO GAIN THE WIZARD'S TRUST, MALIK.
SURELY HE'S SAID SOMETHING ABOUT HIS SECRET MAP OF THE COSMOS.
I WOULD BE MORE THAN HAPPY TO GIVE YOU MORE TIME, BUT I MUST ANSWER TO OUR EMIR, SALADIN, AS MUST WE ALL.
IF I KNEW WHAT YOU WERE TALKING ABOUT, I'D BE MORE THAN HAPPY TO HELP YOU.
BUT I CONFESS THAT I DON'T.
I UNDERSTAND. IT'S ALL RIGHT, SON. YOU CAN GO BACK TO YOUR CELL NOW.
WAIT. I'VE JUST REALIZED. THE WIZARD THINKS WE'VE DRAGGED MALIK HERE AWAY TO BEAT HIM.
HE'D CERTAINLY BE SUSPICIOUS IF HIS CELLMATE RETURNED UNMARKED, NO?

1593.
DON'T FRET. I'LL TAKE GOOD CARE OF YOU.
I ALWAYS DO, BETHANY...
BETHANY...
BETHANY...
BETHANY...

GET IN THERE, YOU. AND GET READY TO TALK.
UHNNGH

SORRY IF I GOT A LITTLE ROUGH THERE, BETHANY.
IT'S ONLY, WELL-- IF THIS CREW OF SPANIARDS KNEW WHERE MY FEALTY TRULY LIES...
STILL, I CAN'T BELIEVE WALSINGHAM SENT YOU. ESPECIALLY AFTER WHAT HAPPENED LAST--
EDMUND?
CLICK

I... BETHANY, YOU HAVEN'T-- NO ONE'S CALLED ME EDMUND IN FOREVER...
YOU NEED TO SEE A DOCTOR.

I'M FINE... I'M FINE. IT'S-- IT FEELS LIKE SOMEONE IS INSIDE MY HEAD.
BUT THAT'S NOT IMPORTANT. WHAT'S IMPORTANT IS... THAT NAUTICAL CHART.

WERE YOU ABLE TO ACQUIRE IT FROM KING PHILIP?
NO. I KNOW WHERE IT IS, THOUGH. BUT I NEED SOMETHING IN RETURN.
WHAT?
I NEED YOU TO GET ME OUT.

MALIK?
MALIK?
THIS IS MALIK, EMIR.
SO... YOU'RE THE ONE WHO'S GOING TO GET THE WIZARD'S CHART FOR ME?
REMEMBER, SALADIN IS NOTHING IF NOT PATIENT--
BUT WITH THE INVADERS EVER THREATENING, EVEN HE KNOWS TIME IS OF THE ESSENCE.
GAIN HIS TRUST, FIND THE LOCATION OF HIS SECRET CHART AND YOU'LL BE HANDSOMELY REWARDED.
FAIL AND, WELL, DON'T THINK YOU CAN'T BE EASILY REPLACED.
AH, MALIK, YOU'RE BACK.
HERE. DRINK THIS.

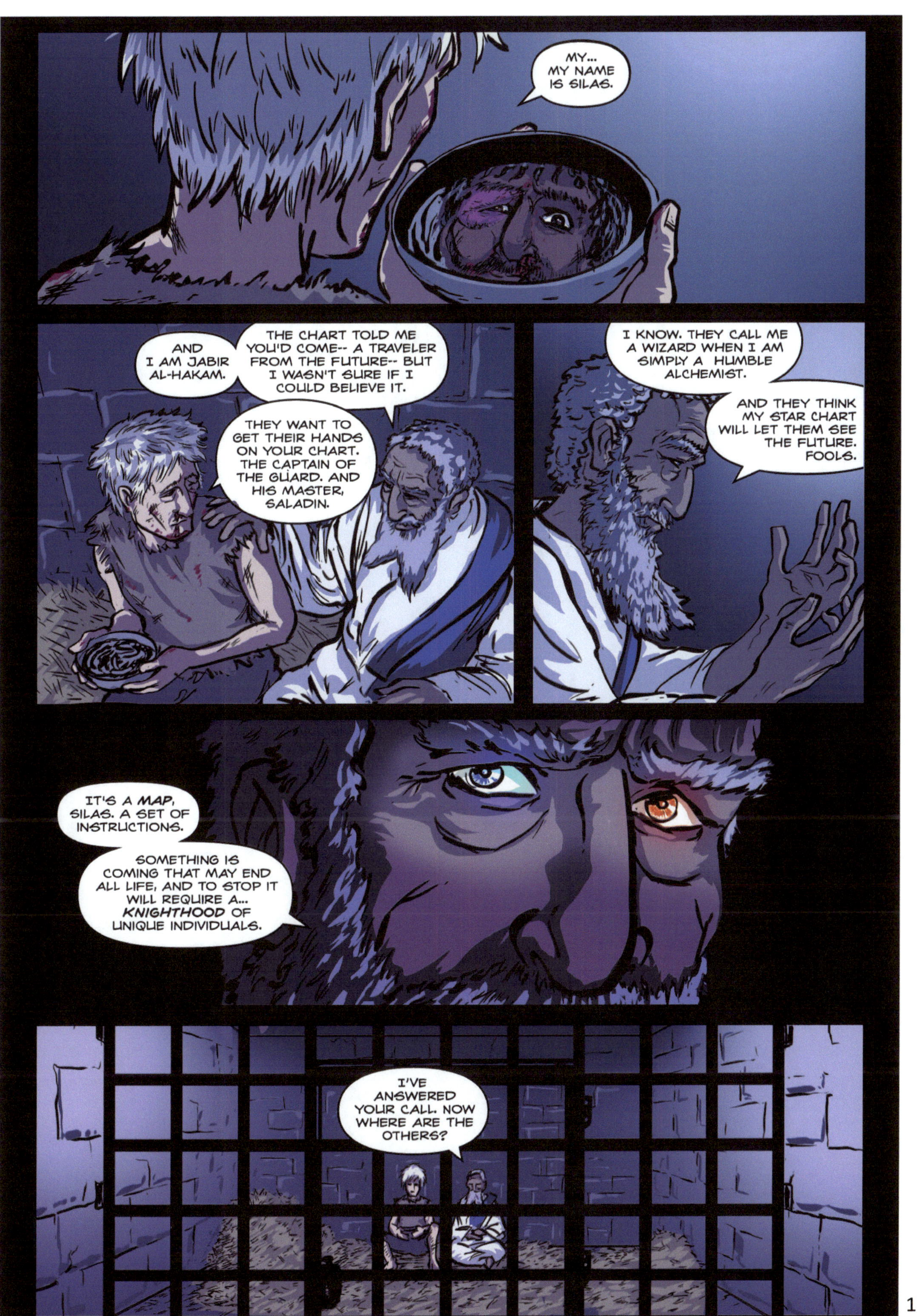

MY... MY NAME IS SILAS.
AND I AM JABIR AL-HAKAM.
THE CHART TOLD ME YOU'D COME-- A TRAVELER FROM THE FUTURE-- BUT I WASN'T SURE IF I COULD BELIEVE IT.
THEY WANT TO GET THEIR HANDS ON YOUR CHART. THE CAPTAIN OF THE GUARD. AND HIS MASTER, SALADIN.
I KNOW. THEY CALL ME A WIZARD WHEN I AM SIMPLY A HUMBLE ALCHEMIST.
AND THEY THINK MY STAR CHART WILL LET THEM SEE THE FUTURE. FOOLS.
IT'S A MAP, SILAS. A SET OF INSTRUCTIONS.
SOMETHING IS COMING THAT MAY END ALL LIFE, AND TO STOP IT WILL REQUIRE A... KNIGHTHOOD OF UNIQUE INDIVIDUALS.
I'VE ANSWERED YOUR CALL. NOW WHERE ARE THE OTHERS?

2022.
UURNGH!
SABOT WAIN
YES, MASTER.
HAVE YOU BEGUN PREPARING THE WAY FOR MY ARRIVAL?
YES, MASTER.
AND THE INFINITY CORE?
THEY ARE NOT PRESENT IN THIS WORLD, MASTER.
NONE SHALL STAND IN YOUR WAY.
GEEK ZODIAC
INFINITY CORE
CHAPTER ONE:
World Enough, and Time
WORDS by James F. Wright
ART by Josh Eckert

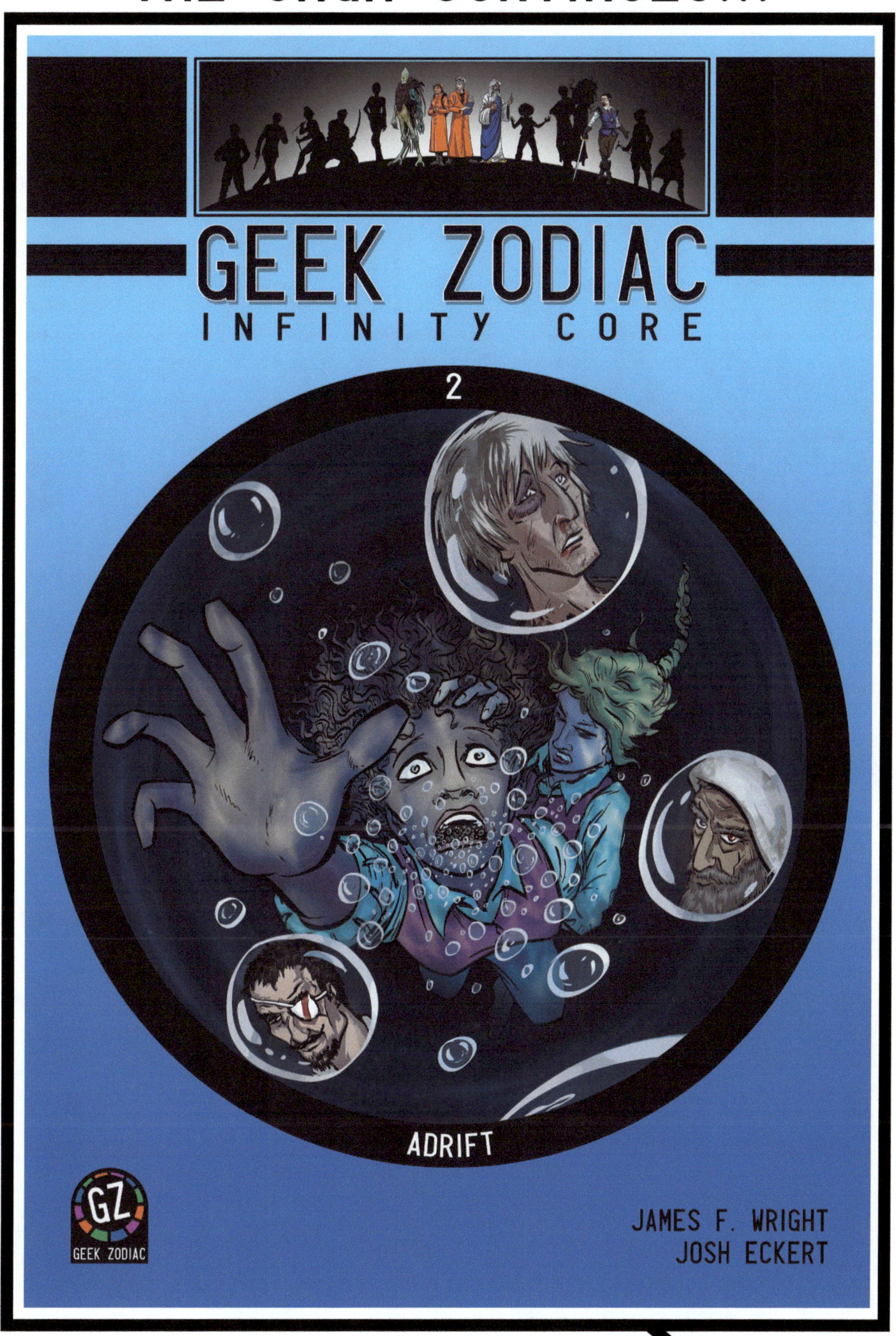
GEEK ZODIAC
INFINITY CORE
2
ADRIFT
GZ
GEEK ZODIAC
JAMES F. WRIGHT
JOSH ECKERT

SKETCHES & DRAFTS

WITH COMMENTARY BY GEEK ZODIAC CO-CREATOR JOSH ECKERT

DESIGNING THE SIGNS

When I first began designing the zodiac signs, the ideas looked like mini-illustrations. I very quickly realized the signs should be more like graphic symbols or glyphs with some illustration elements.

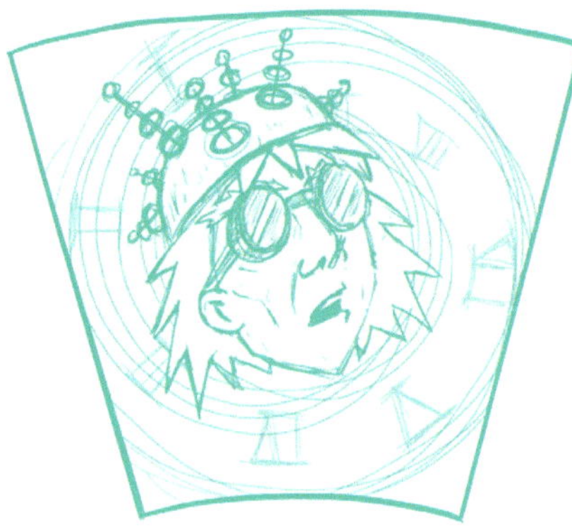

I figured out certain design motifs by designing the signs in pairs. Signs that were placed opposite each other on the zodiac wheel share similar motifs.

For example, the Wizard and Time Traveler signs share a spiral motif. While the Wizard is in control of the spirals, manipulating them with magic, the Time Traveler is at the whim of the spiral, in a state of chaos.

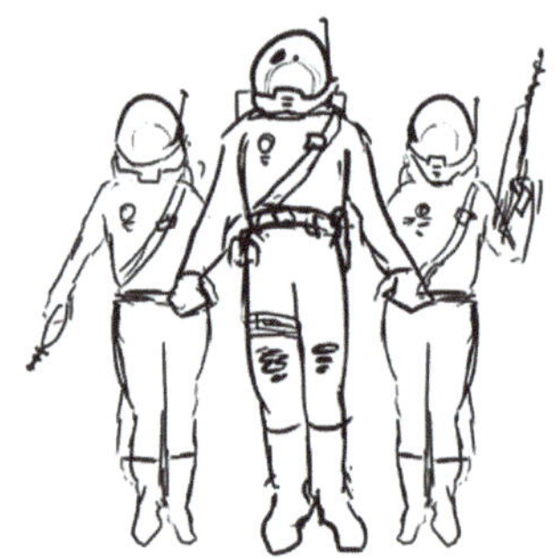

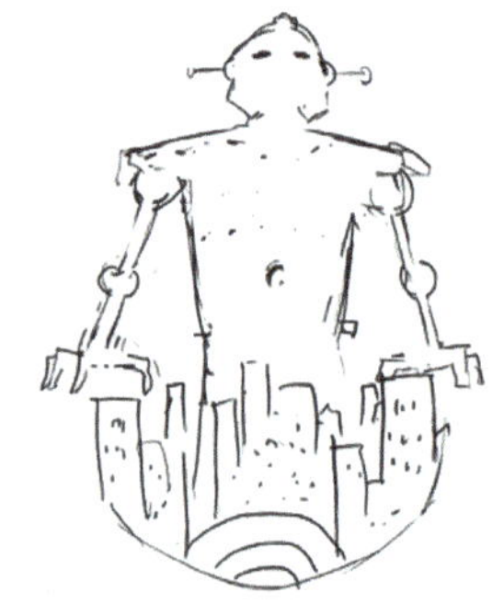

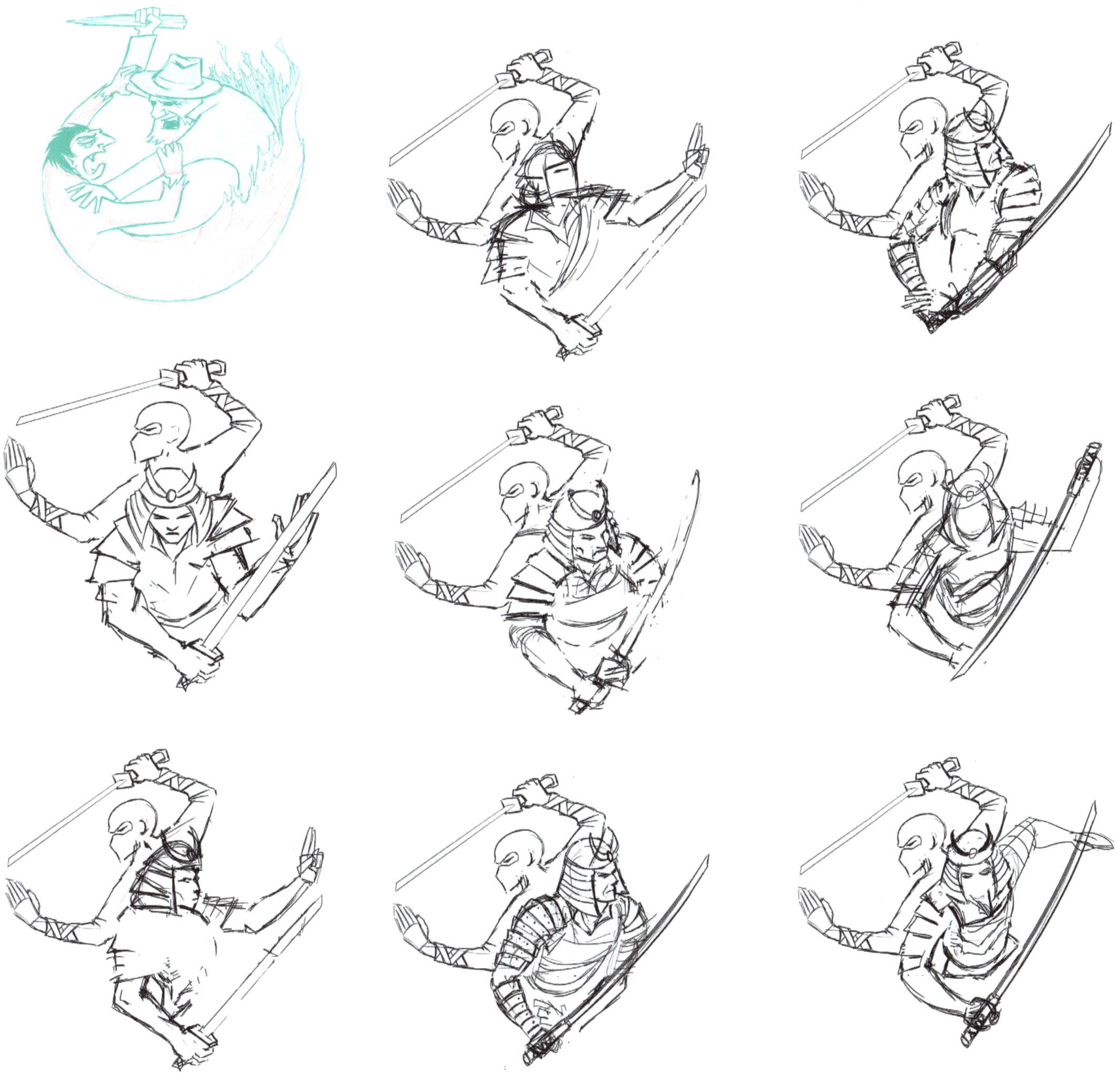

Often one design would come easily to me but its opposite would give me a lot of trouble. The Undead/Slayer design was inspired by the ancient ouroboros symbol depicting a serpent devouring its own tail. As its opposite, I wanted the Ninja/Samurai sign to come across as a more balanced design, but finding the right poses for the figures was a challenge.

The Treasure Hunter and Pirate signs were the last to be designed. It took a while to find a design motif James and I were happy with but when I gave the Treasure Hunter an amulet, the motif became clear: Treasure Hunters take their prizes using their cunning and speed, Pirates take theirs by force.

Because of the shared amulets in these signs, James was inspired to create the ancestral link between the Infinity Core characters Agatha Helstaff and Deadeye.

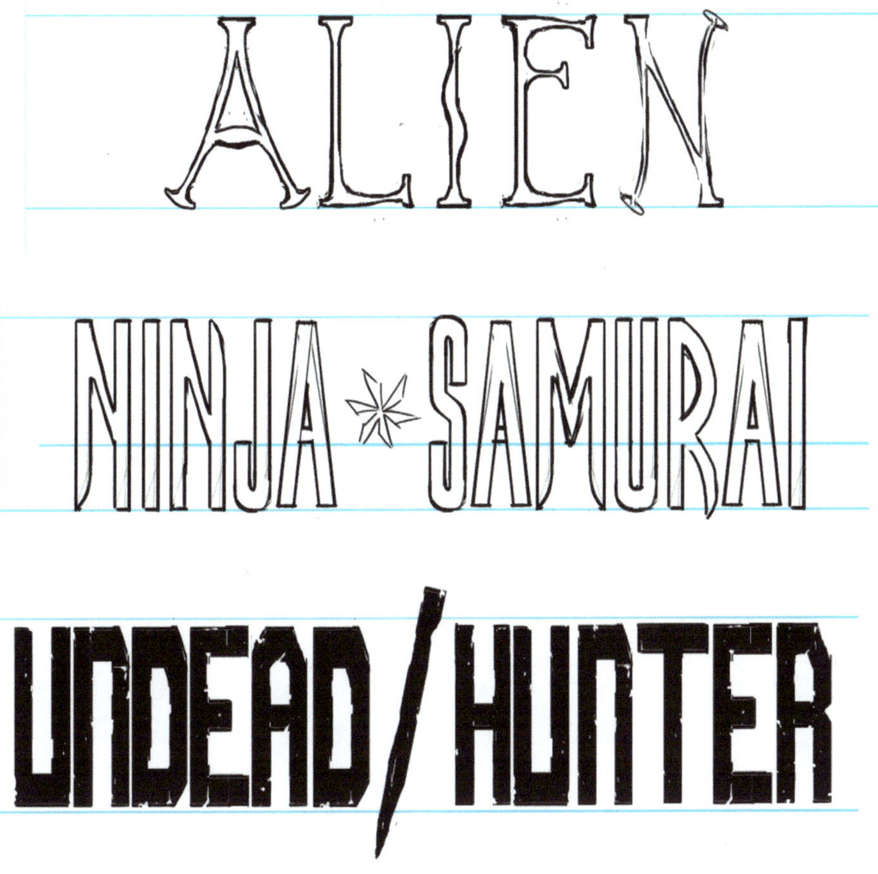

While I was able to find good free fonts for most of the Geek Zodiac signs, the three above were a bit of a challenge. So I opted to design a few fonts of my own.

The Wizard was originally going to be a more traditional Merlin-esque character named Fendritch of Rook's Hollow. But as James began challenging himself to subvert expectations with each of the characters (making the Daikaiju a little girl, the Slayer a rebellious musician, etc.) he thought it better to change the Wizard's country of origin to Egypt in the Middle Ages.

JABIR AL HAKAM
THE WIZARD

Below: Jabir's most trusted students, representing the Four Facets - Akilah, Fatin, Stefanos and Mansur.

MAYOR ABNER PRESENTS AMERICANA WITH THE KEY TO THE CITY!

AMERICANA DEFEATS THE EVIL FRANKENJINN

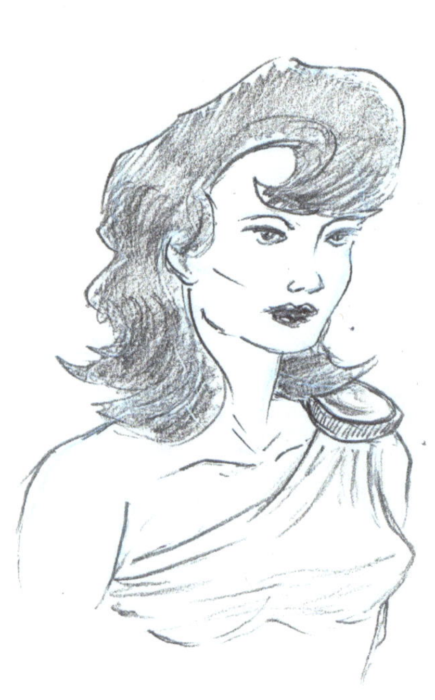

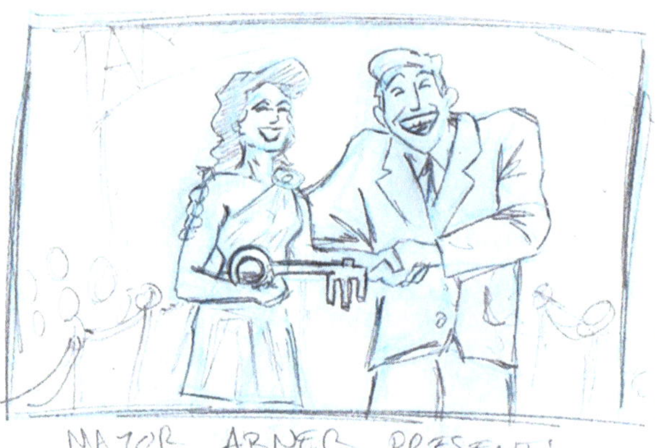

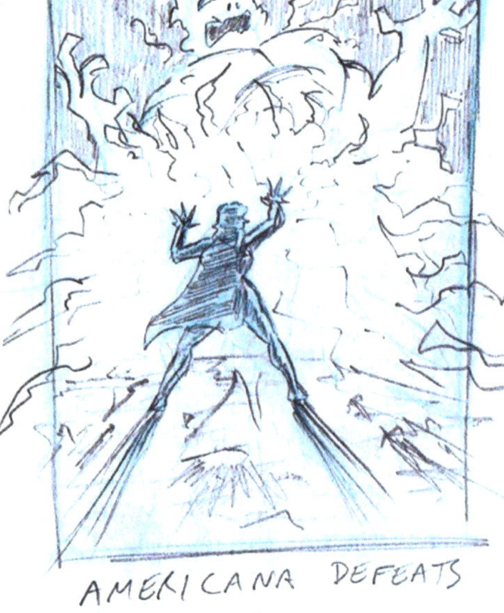

AMERICANA
THE SUPERHERO

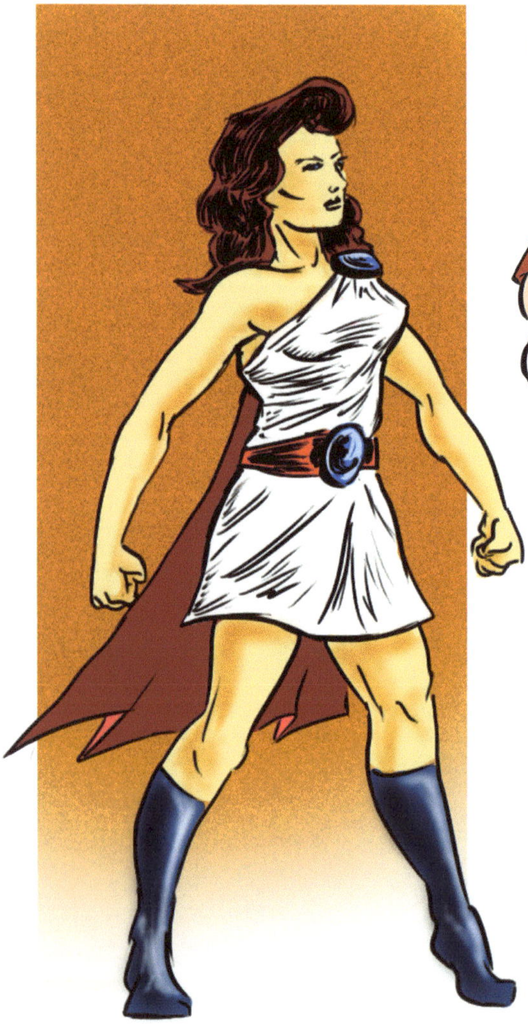

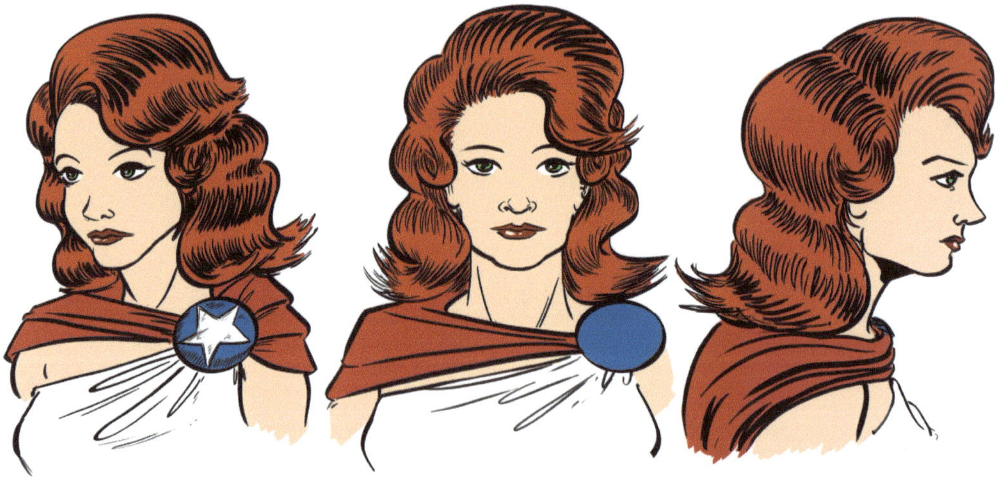

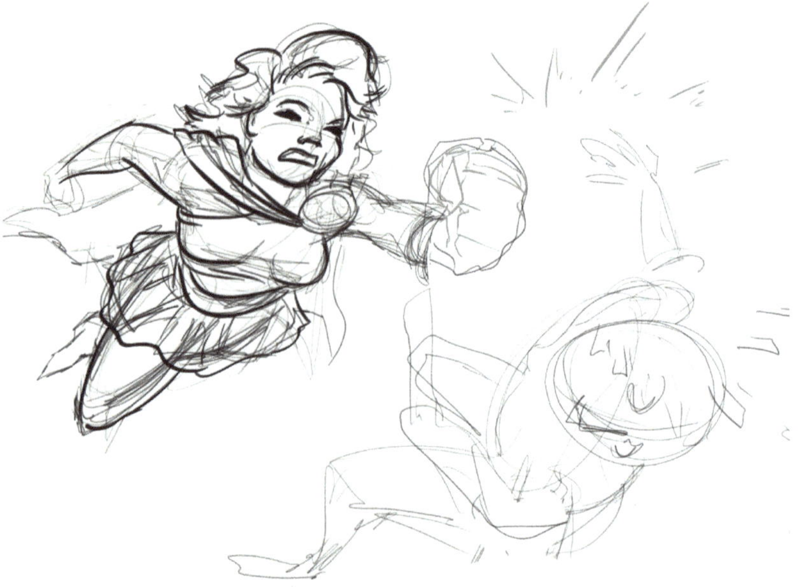

Eventually all of the Infinity Core characters would end up in Silas and Freya's time period (2022), so figuring out how they would adjust their personas outside of their time periods was something James and I were excited to figure out. These drawings of Americana show some of the ways we imagined her adjusting to the future.

DEADEYE
THE PIRATE

AGATHA HELSTAFF
THE TREASURE HUNTER

Credit to my friend and fellow artist, Jackie Crofts for suggesting that Agatha wear a cloche (1930's hat seen at right). Once Agatha had the cloche her look became so much more iconic and James and I really fell for her.

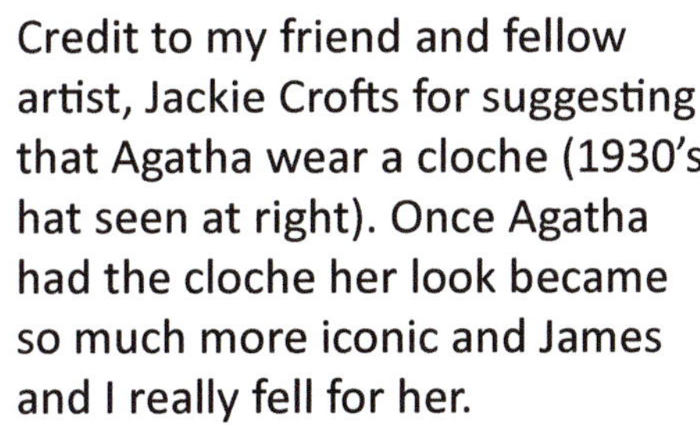

SOSPIRA & LEMUEL
THE UNDEAD and THE SLAYER

Sospira and Lemuel were originally designed to look similar to the Undead/Slayer sign, but as James began began fleshing out their backstory, we opted for a younger and more rebellious pair.

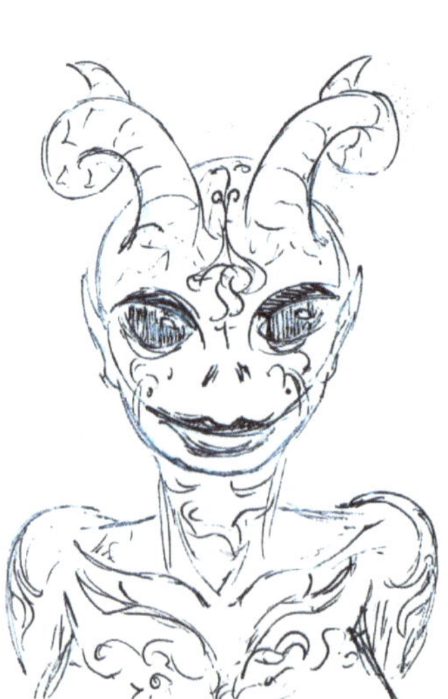

MIRANDA
THE DAIKAIJU

MIRANDA TRANSFORMATION SEQUENCE

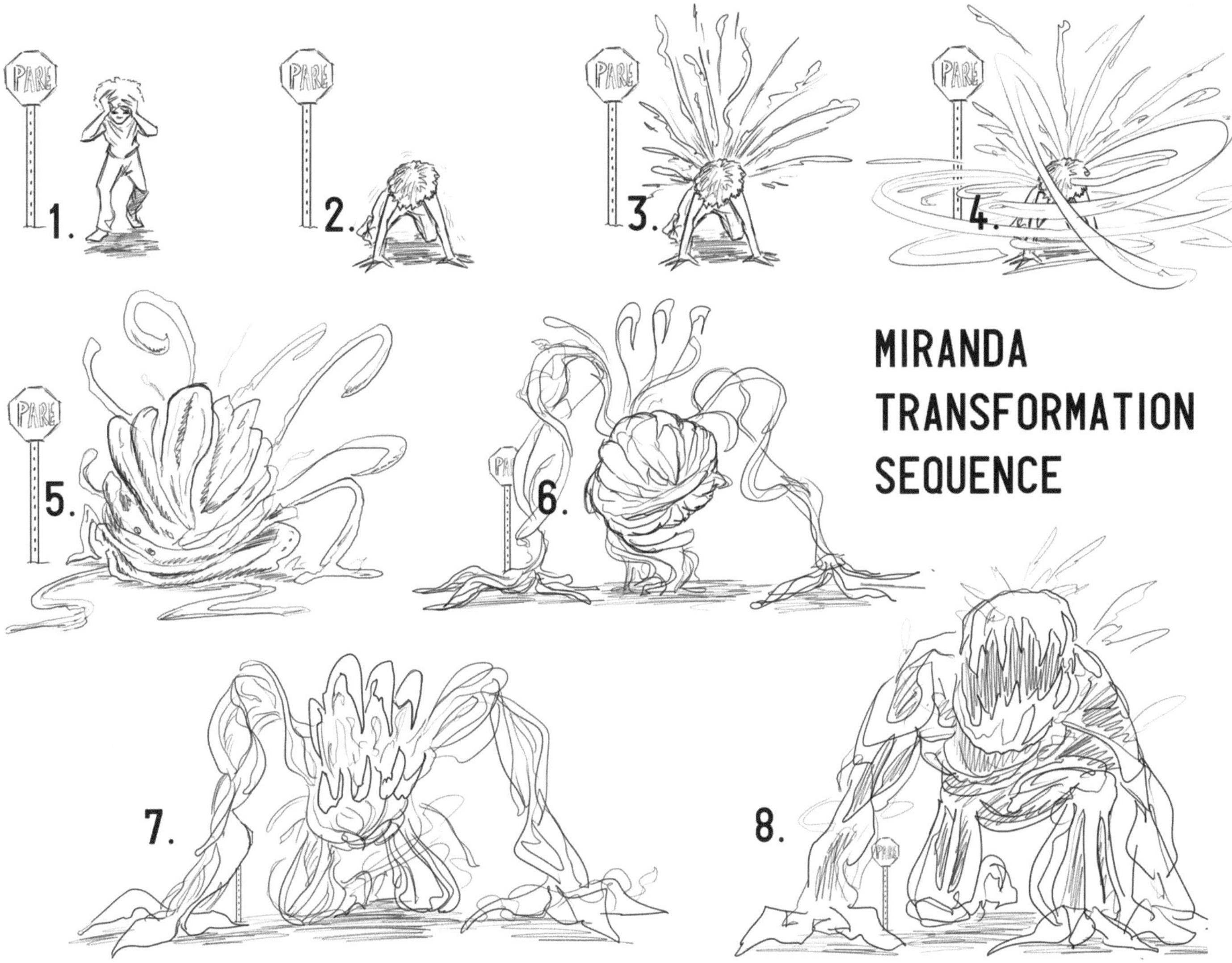

I really wanted Caliban (Miranda's kaiju form) to be pure primal id. I was having a hard time with the design until my friend and fellow artist Kevin Johnson suggested that it shouldn't have eye holes. Then it really clicked.

SILAS AND FREYA
THE TIME TRAVELERS

In early versions of the story, James was thinking the robot character would be a more traditional robot named Friday (seen above) that Silas and Freya built to take care of their child when they weren't around.

I.S.I.S.
THE ROBOT

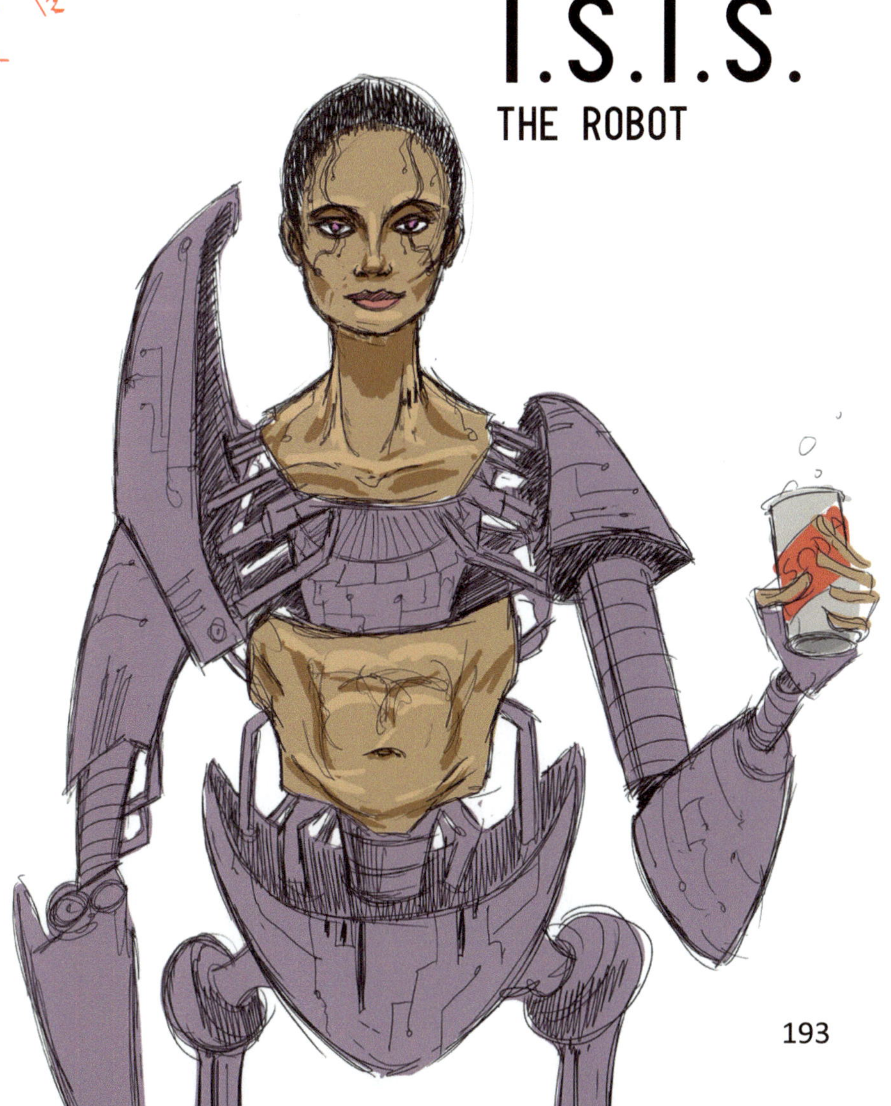

SABOT WAIN
THE ALIEN

My first take on Sabot Wain was a combination of Iggy Pop and David Bowie's character in The Man Who Fell to Earth. But underneath the faux human shell Sabot Wain was actually this bizarre creature seen at right.

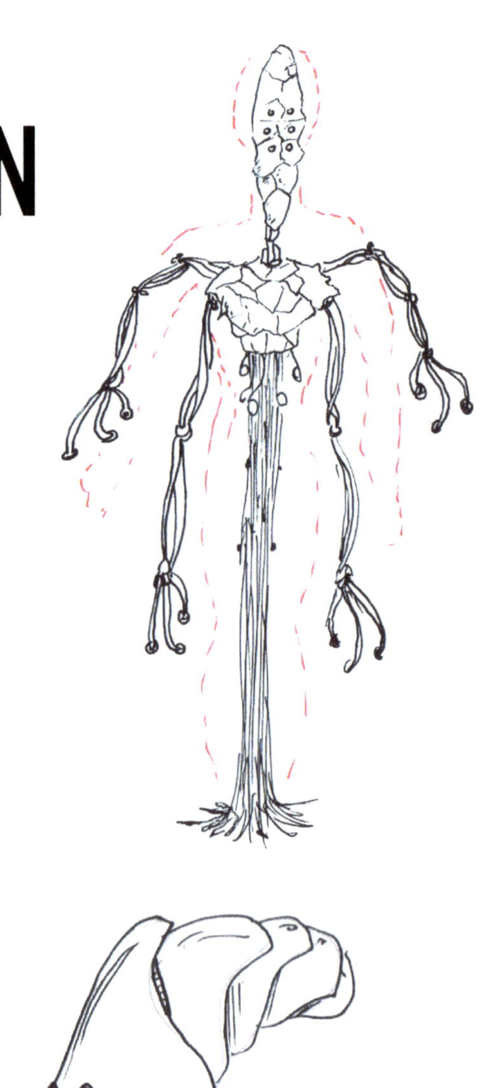

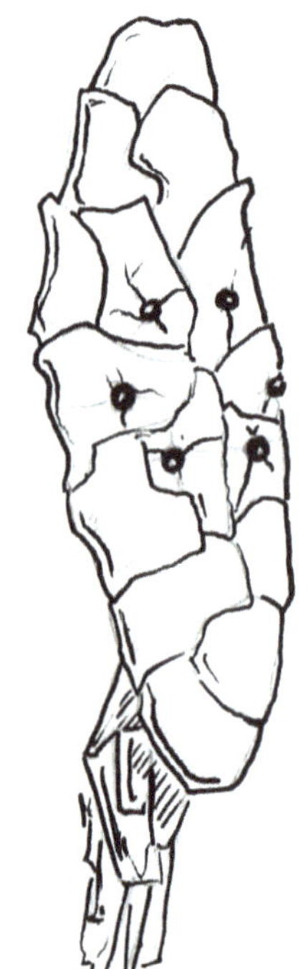

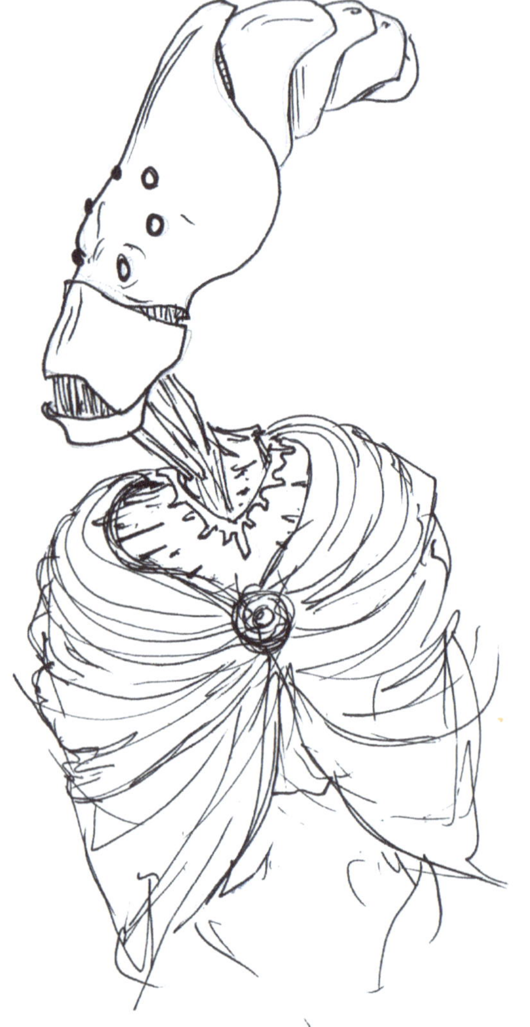

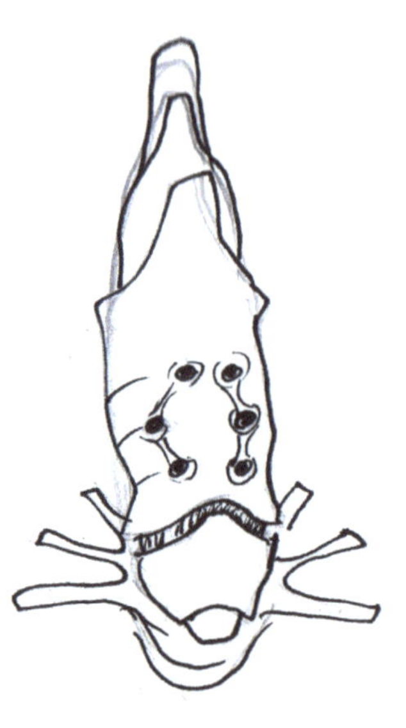

The Alien was a real problem for us early on. In one take on the story, the alien was actually Freya, transformed in the timestream by an alien consciousness trying to warn Earth of the Entrope's approach.

Coming up with a look that seemed alien enough, yet also referenced Freya was quite a challenge. Though I eventually wore James down on the Sabot Wain design you see in Infinity Core #1, I think deep down he would've preferred the design below.

Behold the Page of Shame, devoted to the four characters who are the most criminally underdeveloped, design-wise. These are the least embarrassing old sketches I could find of these guys.

HOTARU & HISAKAGE
THE NINJA & THE SAMURAI

GABRIEL GRIMES
THE ASTRONAUT

Grimes experienced very little design attention because once James and I saw a picture of astrophysicist Neil DeGrasse Tyson as a young man sporting an afro and some 1970s sideburns, we knew we'd found our Astronaut.

ELIOT SPHINX
THE SPY

THE ENTROPE

MAKING COMICS

James F. Wright
[redacted].com

PAGE 1:

[_Note: As ever, these are merely suggestions; how I see it in my mind. Feel free to let me know if you have a better idea of how to present something or, hell, just do it and we'll work it out._]

ONE (splash):
The outskirts of a VILLAGE in the Italian countryside circa late 19th Century. A MOB of angry villagers, in full climax-of-_Frankenstein_, torches-and-pitchforks mode chase THREE WOMEN in cloaks out of the village and into the surrounding FOREST.

1 CAPTION:	Northern Italy. Late 19th Century.
2 CAPTION/Esmerelda:	"Have I ever told you the story of the <u>Sisters of Sorrow</u>, child?
3 CAPTION/Esmerelda:	"Eight years ago, three Roma sisters--healers all--were betrayed by the very people they once served.
4 CAPTION/Esmerelda:	"Few things stir up a mob like a tragedy. And a woman to blame it on."

TWO (inset):
Close on CORDELIA, 27, the eldest of the three sisters, running while looking back over her shoulder, afraid.

5 CAPTION/Esmerelda:	"There was beautiful <u>Cordelia</u>, the eldest.
6 CAPTION/Esmerelda:	"A rumored <u>succubus</u> charged with ensorcelling the virtuous."

THREE (inset):
Close on LUCIA, 26, the second eldest of the three sisters, running, her eyes cast downward, demure.

7 CAPTION/Esmerelda:	"Melancholy <u>Lucia</u>, the middle sister.
8 CAPTION/Esmerelda:	"Branded a <u>banshee</u> and accused of driving stalwart men to despair."

FOUR (inset):
Close on ESMERELDA, 25, the youngest, running. But unlike her sisters, she's facing front, determined and defiant despite those who would do her harm.

9 CAPTION/Esmerelda:	"And, finally, imperious Esmerelda, the youngest.
10 CAPTION/Esmerelda:	"Accused of <u>witchcraft</u> and killing the harvest."

COMIC BOOK ART BOARD
The Continuum:
Soul Survivor   3   1   10-9-11   Josh Ecker
199

DIGITAL INKS BY KEVIN JOHNSON

PAGES 2-3:

[*Note: Two-page spread. Awww, yeah! Despite being a two-page spread, this is intended to be more like* Silas's *penultimate page rather than* Deadeye's *action-packed two-pager. By which I mean, aside from* Panels One *and* Twelve-Fourteen, *they don't flow in a chronological order but are more like glimpses from* Agatha's *progress through the labyrinth.*]

ONE:
AGATHA steps across the THRESHOLD of the labyrinth's entrance, silhouetted by the sun from outside. In one hand she holds her coiled ROPE and GRAPPLING HOOK.

NO COPY.

TWO:
AGATHA turns a STONE WHEEL with all her might, droplets of sweat forming on her brow.

NO COPY.

THREE:
AGATHA jumps straight up as a pair of AXES on hinges swing at her, slamming into the space she's just vacated.

1 SFX/Axes on wall: SHINNNG

FOUR:
AGATHA swims deep under the water toward us.

NO COPY.

FIVE:
AGATHA inches her way along a dangerously narrow LEDGE, her back to the wall.

NO COPY.

SIX:
AGATHA climbs toward us up the rope attached to her GRAPPLING HOOK, which is affixed to a small promontory. Below her we can just make out the floor of hard, iron spikes.

NO COPY.

SEVEN:
AGATHA covers herself as best she can with her JACKET as a legion of BATS fly screeching at her.

2 SFX/Bats: Skreeee Skreeee

EIGHT:
AGATHA crawls through a tight crevasse as SCORPIONS crawl along—and on top of—her.

NO COPY.

202

PAGES 2-3 (CONT.)

NINE:
AGATHA ducks just in the nick of time, managing to keep her hat on, as a burst of FLAME spews above her.

3 SFX/Flame: FWOOSH

TEN:
AGATHA hangs by her fingertips, making her way across another narrow LEDGE, as ALLIGATORS snap at her dangling feet from below.

NO COPY.

ELEVEN:
AGATHA, hanging slothlike from her outstretched ROPE, pulls herself across a wide expanse.

NO COPY.

TWELVE:
AGATHA stands before a wall made up of stone TILES, each with a hieroglyphic etched onto it, illuminated by the TORCH she now holds. AGATHA pushes one of the stone TILES.

4 SFX/Tile: Click.

THIRTEEN:
A theretofore unseen DOOR slides open.

5 SFX/Door: SHUNNK

FOURTEEN:
AGATHA stands in the threshold of the now-open door, leading to the SANCTUM OF THE MORNING.

6 AGATHA: Esteban!

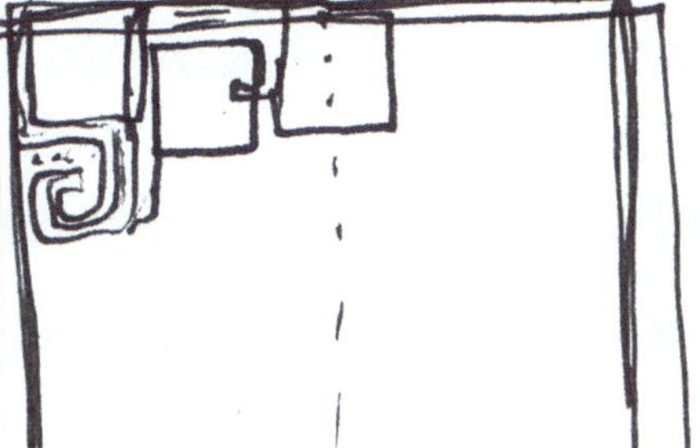

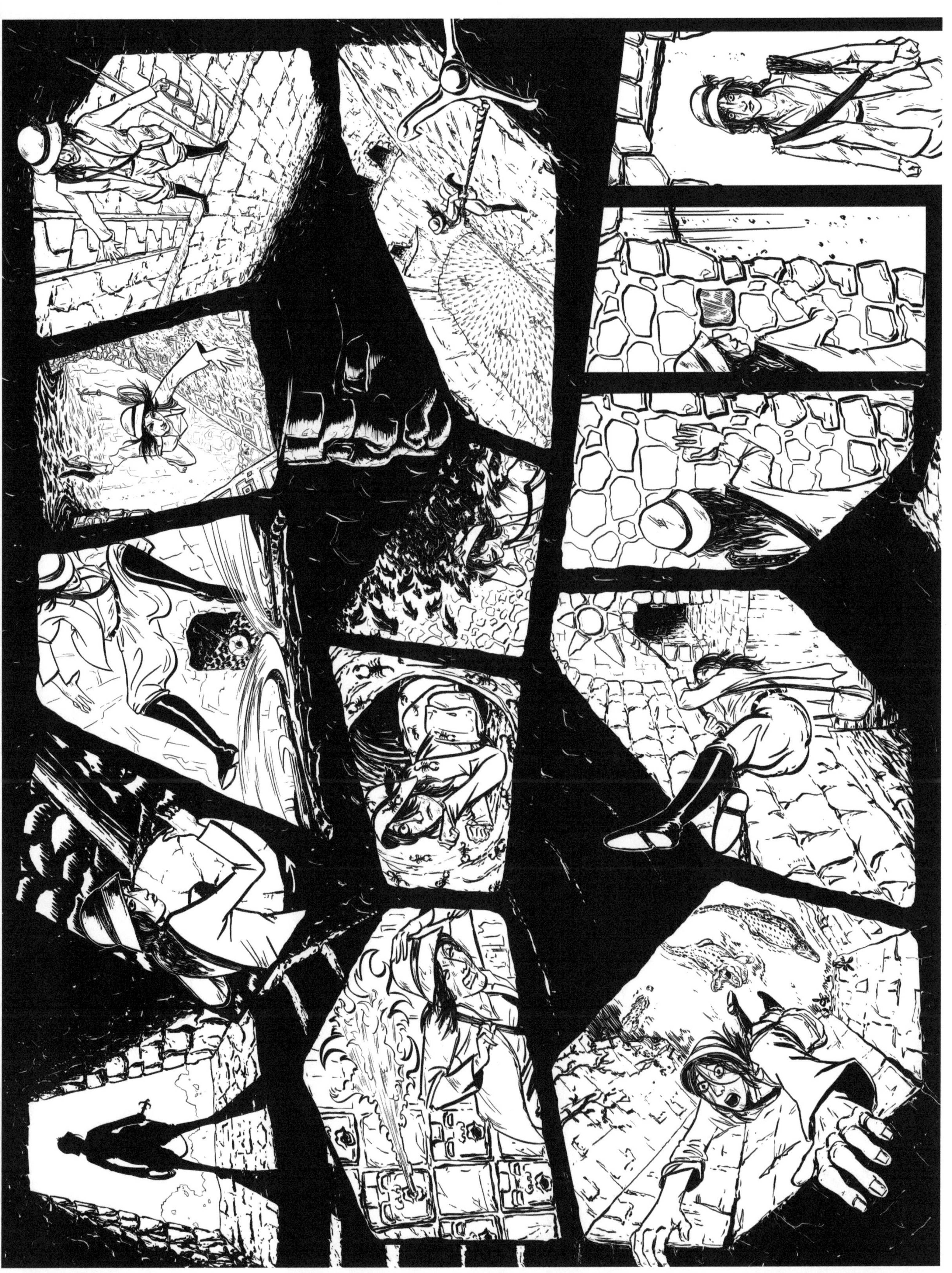

PAGE 7

<u>ONE:</u>
Close on the RUBBLE of the now-destroyed CAPP Facility.

NO COPY.

<u>TWO:</u>
Pulling back a little farther from the WRECKAGE, we see two pairs of UNDAMAGED FEET, standing there. Silas's and Freya's.

NO COPY.

<u>THREE:</u>
Pulling back a little farther, SILAS and FREYA stand with their backs to us, their respective AURAS dancing and intermingling about. Not a single hair on their heads has been harmed, nor their clothing or any aspect of them. Silas turns to face Freya. Freya, meanwhile, looks back over her shoulder (toward us) at something off-panel and her eyes go wide.

1 SILAS: What-- What happened to us?
2 FREYA: I don't know, Silas, but that might have the answer.

<u>FOUR:</u>
In the debris where the Continuum Collider once stood now stands a PORTAL, undulating softly and emitting ORANGE, BLUE, GREEN and PURPLE LIGHT in waves.

NO COPY.

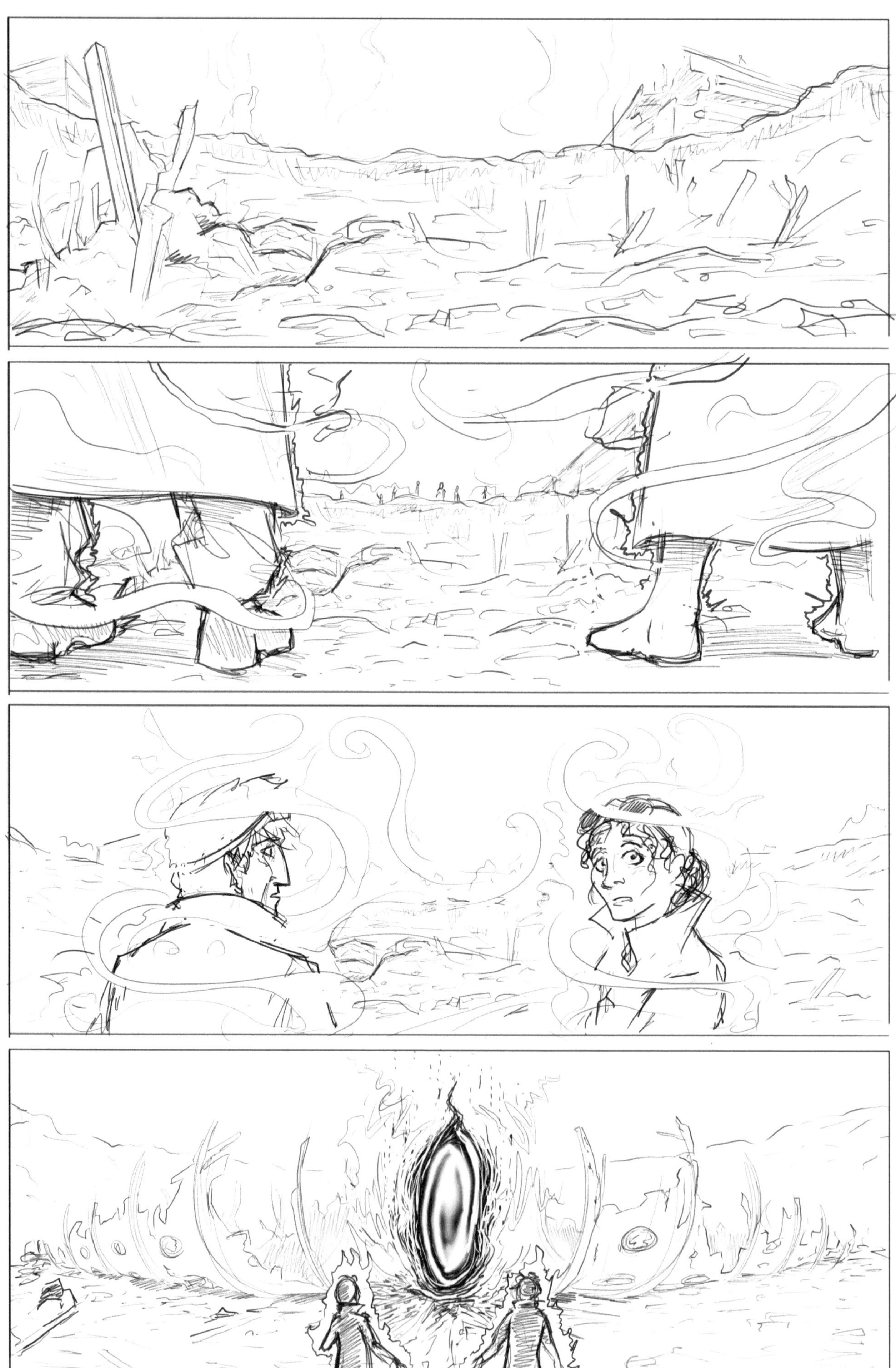

Before it was called
Infinity Core, we
experimented
with a lot of dif-
ferent titles and
title designs for the
comic.

Ultimately these
titles were not
available for us to
use.

When James and I put the webcomic on a holiday hiatus in the winter of 2011-2012, I made this promo image in the spring of 2012 to announce the return of The Continuum prologue comics. At the time, we had only revealed four of the fourteen characters, but I put some little trinkets in the picture to hint at each of the remaining characters.

An early version of the
Undead/Slayer pair,
Lemuel and Sospira.

GEEK ZODIAC
INFINITY CORE

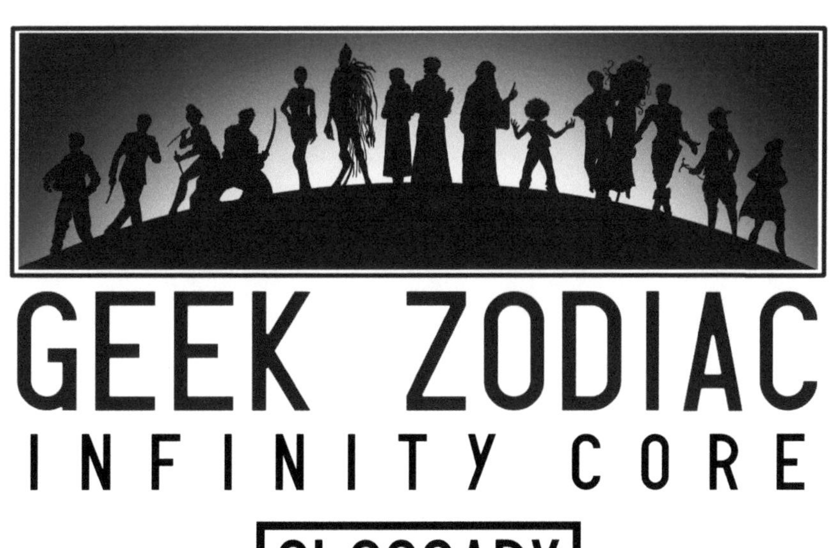

GLOSSARY

The Infinity Core - The collective name for the four empyrean particles of existence--Fighter, Scholar, Rogue and Stranger. Time travelers Drs. Silas and Freya Strickland were bombarded with these particles, giving them the ability to travel through time. The Infinity Core is also, collectively, the only thing capable of stopping the reality-destroying entity known as the Entrope.

Fighter - The facet of existence related to the areas of combat and defense, the aspect of the body, the element of earth, and the blood type A, all of which emerge from the Fighter particle of the Infinity Core.

Scholar - The facet of existence related to the areas of wisdom and knowledge, the aspect of the mind, the element of air, and the blood type AB, all of which emerge from the Scholar particle of the Infinity Core.

Rogue - The facet of existence related to the areas of cunning and daring, the aspect of the spirit, the element of fire, and the blood type B, all of which emerge from the Rogue particle of the Infinity Core.

Stranger - The facet of existence related to the areas of empathy and understanding, the aspect of the soul, the element of water, and the blood type O, all of which emerge from the Stranger particle of the Infinity Core.

The Passage - The time portal through which the alien Sabot Wain arrives in our universe. This is initially the way that Drs. Silas and Freya Strickland travel through time to gather the other members of the Infinity Core.

The Inhabitance Effect - The physical effect allowing time travelers Drs. Freya and Silas Strickland to inhabit the body of another person in the time period into which they time travel.

Transference – The phenomenon by which Dr. Freya or Silas Strickland, should they die while inhabiting the body of another person in the past, will find their consciousness passed on to the next person in the Infinity Core cycle, while the body they inhabited previously perishes. Until they have gathered all the necessary members of the Infinity Core, they cannot return to their present of 2022 and end the cycle.

CAPP - The **C**enter for **A**pplied **P**article **P**hysics, the lab where Drs. Silas and Freya Strickland work.

Time Dilation - The effect by which time in the present era passes more slowly than in a past era. For example, when Silas or Freya travel back in time, a month might pass during the period to which they travel, while in their home era of 2022, perhaps only a single day will have passed. Quantum Entanglement – When Silas or Freya enters The Passage to travel back in time, some of their quantum essence, made up of the empyrean particles, remains in the present of 2022 as a tether. So, when their mission is complete and they have gathered all the members of the Infinity Core, they will be pulled through time and space by their tether in 2022.

The Entrope - An entity of darkness and shadow born at the Big Bang and the antithesis of The Infinity core. It seeks to return existence to a pre-Big Bang state of nothingness by destroying all universes.

The Emissaries – Four otherworldly agents subservient to The Entrope. The Emissaries are tasked with seeking out and preparing universes for destruction at the hands of The Entrope. Legend has it that these were the first four beings to stand against The Entrope, but after falling to it they were forced into serving the dark entity. Though they are incapable of acting in direct opposition to their master, one of them—Sabot Wain—has specifically sought out worlds abundant in empyrean particles in hopes that there will be heroes there who can stop The Entrope once and for all.

Entropy – Defined for our purposes as the constant state of decay within a given system—the multiverse—as that system hurtles toward a state of thermodynamic equilibrium (heat death) and the end of all life. That which we call The Entrope is the physical manifestation of this property, and its procession comes in four stages of entropy: Celestial, Environmental, Genetic and Social.

Celestial Entropy (Stage 1) – The first wave of The Entrope's procession, Celestial Entropy is measured in eons and epochs. It results in the deaths of stars and suns, and the proliferation of asteroids and other destructive celestial bodies.

Environmental Entropy (Stage 2) – The second wave of The Entrope's procession, Environmental Entropy is the effect of meteorological and natural disasters on a universe. These include, but are not limited to, volcanic eruptions, tsunamis, earthquakes and hurricanes, as well as famine and drought.

Genetic Entropy (Stage 3) – The third wave of The Entrope's procession affects the genetic material of organisms of the targeted universe. Homogeneity is in keeping with the nature of The Entrope, and the mixing of diverse genetic material slows the entity's procession.

Social Entropy (Stage 4) – The fourth wave of The Entrope's procession, Social Entropy is the breakdown of the social system, or civilization. Crime, war, violence, mistrust and ennui. This procession sees the rise of dictators and despots, the emergence of police and surveillance states, and an improved efficiency with which organisms can destroy one another.

Free Comic Book Day
May 4th, 2013

ABOUT THE AUTHORS

James F. Wright was instilled with a love of reading by his schoolteacher mom and a love of reading comics by his Superman-fan dad, eventually branching out into Spider-Man and the New Mutants. A child of the '80s, he and his friends grew up loving the Ninja Turtles and the Transformers, as well as Indiana Jones, Blade Runner and Aliens, all of which laid the groundwork for what would become the Geek Zodiac. His passion for comics has remained constant, and when he's not writing comics (in his free time), he's thinking about them. His favorite comic book characters are Black Bolt, Kitty Pryde, Saturn Girl and Kagehisa Anotsu. He loves pie and lives in Los Angeles.

wordsthatfit.tumblr.com

Josh Eckert is an illustrator and graphic designer. Whether he makes it into the professional comics industry or not, you can be absolutely sure he'll still be making comics somehow. He lives in Indianapolis, Indiana, with his wife-to-be and daughter-on-the-way. He sustains himself on a steady diet of cereal, peanut butter, and Coen brothers films.

josheckert.com